Jaws of the Dinosaur

Suddenly, the head and long neck of the Apatosaurus swung down, and it began opening and closing its mechanical jaws. "Wow," Frank said under his breath. It really did look lifelike. He went outside for a closer look.

Just then, the neck of the Apatosaurus swept down, and Frank gasped. The huge head knocked Parker off his feet with a violent blow. Then its jaws opened and closed again, gripping Joe around the waist in a firm, quick motion.

As Joe let out a surprised cry, waving his arms and legs around frantically, the massive dinosaur lifted him high into the air!

The Hardy Boys Mystery Stories

#59	Night of the Werewolf	#96	Wipeout
#60	Mystery of the Samurai Sword	#97	Cast of Criminals
#61	The Pentagon Spy	#98	Spark of Suspicion
#62	The Apeman's Secret	#99	Dungeon of Doom
#63	The Mummy Case	#100	The Secret of the Island Treasure
#64	Mystery of Smugglers Cove		
#65	The Stone Idol	#101	The Money Hunt
#66	The Vanishing Thieves	#102	Terminal Shock
#67	The Outlaw's Silver	#103	The Million-Dollar Nightmare
#68	Deadly Chase	#104	Tricks of the Trade
#69	The Four-headed Dragon	#105	The Smoke Screen Mystery
#70	The Infinity Clue	#106	Attack of the Video Villains
#71	Track of the Zombie	#107	Panic on Gull Island
#72	The Voodoo Plot	#108	Fear on Wheels
#73	The Billion Dollar Ransom	#109	The Prime-Time Crime
#74	Tic-Tac-Terror	#110	The Secret of Sigma Seven
#75	Trapped at Sea	#111	Three-Ring Terror
#76	Game Plan for Disaster	#112	The Demolition Mission
#77	The Crimson Flame	#113	Radical Moves
#78	Cave-in!	#114	The Case of the Counterfeit Criminals
#79	Sky Sabotage		
#80	The Roaring River Mystery	#115	Sabotage at Sports City
#81	The Demon's Den	#116	Rock 'n' Roll Renegades
#82	The Blackwing Puzzle	#117	The Baseball Card Conspiracy
#83	The Swamp Monster		
#84	Revenge of the Desert Phantom	#118	Danger in the Fourth Dimension
#85	The Skyfire Puzzle	#119	Trouble at Coyote Canyon
#86	The Mystery of the Silver Star	#120	The Case of the Cosmic Kidnapping
#87	Program for Destruction		
#88	Tricky Business	#121	The Mystery in the Old Mine
#89	The Sky Blue Frame	#122	Carnival of Crime
#90	Danger on the Diamond	#123	The Robot's Revenge
#91	Shield of Fear	#124	Mystery with a Dangerous Beat
#92	The Shadow Killers	#125	Mystery on Makatunk Island
#93	The Serpent's Tooth Mystery	#126	Racing to Disaster
#94	Breakdown in Axeblade	#127	Reel Thrills
#95	Danger on the Air	#128	Day of the Dinosaur

Available from MINSTREL Books

THE HARDY BOYS® MYSTERY STORIES

128

The HARDY BOYS®

DAY OF THE DINOSAUR

FRANKLIN W. DIXON

A MINSTREL® BOOK

PUBLISHED BY POCKET BOOKS

New York   London   Toronto   Sydney   Tokyo   Singapore

A MINSTREL PAPERBACK *Original*

A Minstrel Book published by
POCKET BOOKS, a division of Simon & Schuster Inc.
1230 Avenue of the Americas, New York, NY 10020

Copyright © 1994 by Simon & Schuster Inc.
Front cover illustration by Vince Natale
Produced by Mega-Books of New York, Inc.

ISBN: 0-671-87212-5

First Minstrel Books printing October 1994

10 9 8 7 6 5 4 3 2 1

Printed in the U.S.A.

Contents

1.	Sparks Fly!	1
2.	A Surprising Threat	16
3.	Heads Up!	21
4.	Up in the Air	33
5.	Danger: Triceratops Crossing	44
6.	A Disappearing Dinosaur	56
7.	Fossil Fiasco	66
8.	A Crushing Case	74
9.	Night Prowlers	81
10.	Out of Control!	93
11.	Over the Edge	105
12.	An After-Hours Intruder	115
13.	Caught in the Act	122
14.	A Prehistoric Trap	136
15.	Cover-Up Uncovered	145

DAY OF THE DINOSAUR

1 Sparks Fly!

"Don't look now," Frank Hardy whispered, "but I think that's a dinosaur peeking over those trees." His younger brother, Joe, stopped and gawked. Sure enough, a large reptilian head on a snaky neck loomed over the treetops.

For a second, Joe's blue eyes went wide. Then he glared at his brother. "You've been watching too many horror movies," he said. "That may be an apatosaurus, but it's not going anywhere."

Frank grinned. "Okay, so it's a replica, but you'll have to admit it was real enough to get you going for a second."

The brothers stood at the gate of a slightly run-down estate on the outskirts of their hometown of Bayport. The main building—an old mansion—

1

was hidden by a grove of trees, beyond which the apatosaurus stood silent guard.

"When this new museum is finished, it will be top-notch," Joe said. "My biology teacher can't stop talking about it."

Frank stared in surprise. "You mean you actually listened to your biology teacher?"

"Ha-ha," Joe said, rolling his eyes. He peered down the entrance drive. "I wonder when it's going to open."

"Can you wait two weeks?" a female voice said behind them.

Frank and Joe whirled to see a smiling young woman walk up. She was tall and slim, and her long, dark hair hung in a braid down her back. As she came closer, a surprised look came over her face.

"Frank and Joe Hardy!" she exclaimed.

At the same time Frank smiled in recognition. "Sally Jenkins," he said, putting out a hand. "How is your dad?" Mr. Jenkins sometimes worked on investigations with the boys' father, Fenton Hardy. The two detectives saw a lot of each other. But Frank and Joe hadn't seen Sally in years.

Sally shook Frank's hand and then reached for Joe's. "I'm just fine. What brings the two of you here—to my home away from home?"

Frank nodded toward his younger brother. "Joe's been dying to check out the prehistory museum complex." Joe shot Frank a look and Frank quickly added, "Okay, okay, I've been a bit curious myself.

2

We both have a free period for our last class, so we decided to stop by today." Eighteen-year-old Frank was a senior, while Joe was a junior.

"What do you mean, your 'home away from home'?" Joe asked Sally.

Sally gestured with the clipboard in her left hand to an area beyond the mansion cluttered with trucks, workers, and construction materials. "With the opening only two weeks away and so much left to be done, I seem to put in twenty-four-hour days. I'm the assistant exhibitions director here," she explained.

Frank raised his eyebrows in admiration, and Sally quickly added, "It's a fancy title, but only a title. Right now I'm doing a little bit of everything —mainly overseeing the final construction and installations."

Joe's eyes brightened suddenly. "Sally, I know you're not open yet, but could we go in and take a quick look around—at least at that apatosaurus?"

Sally checked her watch. "I'm due for a break. Let's squeeze in a quick tour."

"That would be great," Frank said. "Thanks, Sally."

"I'll just stop by the office and let my director know where I am. Come on, we'll take the employees' entrance."

Sally led the way around the side of the mansion to an unmarked door. Inside, the boys could see that one wing of the old building had been con-

3

verted to offices. Sally dashed into a room and reappeared a few minutes later without her clipboard.

"These used to be the kitchens," she said with a grin. "Mr. Sackville left us his mansion and his collection, along with a bit of seed money. But it's a lot of work starting a museum from scratch. Wait till you see what we did to the old ballroom."

Sally opened a door and led Frank and Joe along a curving hallway. "As you can see, the outside wall is made up of a series of large displays," she began. "In each, we've created a prehistoric panorama, complete with a painted landscape that we hope looks as if it's stretching into the distance."

"Whoa," Joe said, peering into the first case, ignoring the sounds of pounding hammers and electric saws in the distance. "What's this?"

"That shows the Precambrian period, when the surface of the earth was mostly pools of bubbling lava and the atmosphere, methane and water vapor," Sally said.

Frank squinted. "I can barely tell where the foreground ends and the painting begins."

"That's the idea," Sally said. She moved on. "Here's the later Precambrian, when the first single-celled organisms started developing in the earliest seas."

Inside the exhibit, a worker put finishing touches on a background painting of a dark, cloudy sky. He turned and waved to Sally as they went by.

"That's Michael Murray," Sally said when they

4

passed. "He's not only an artist, but a doctoral candidate in archeology at the university. Many of our workers have volunteered their services as part of their graduate studies."

Sally led Frank and Joe from one display to another, each a step forward in time. Workers were painting, building, or cleaning in many of them. The boys got a quick look at the Paleozoic, when the first reptiles appeared, then the Mesozoic, when the dinosaurs took over, and finally, the Cenozoic, when mammals appeared.

Frank stared at each display, completely fascinated. "This is impressive work, Sally."

"Thanks," Sally said. "I'm sure Dr. Smith, our director, will be pleased to hear you say that. We've just covered five billion years in a little over five minutes, by the way. Now over here, in the center of the hall, we have a depiction of the emergence of humans only a few million years ago."

Sally led them from the outer wall to the center of the hall, where there were life-sized figures of humans at various stages of evolution. They were grouped around campfires, standing at the entrances to caves, and walking on seemingly vast plains with herds of animals such as woolly mammoths far in the distance. In front of the last exhibit, the boys saw several cases filled with primitive stone axes and arrowheads.

One case held a three-foot-wide square of clay carved to show an ancient bison. The animal seemed to jut from the surface, amazingly alive.

5

"This is one of our most important pieces," Sally said proudly. "It was made by a Cro-Magnon artist some fifteen thousand years ago and was found in a cave in southern France."

Frank stepped closer. "Awesome. Some guy thousands of years ago actually made that."

Sally smiled. "That's the extraordinary thing about an original piece. The sense of history is so powerful. It's just not the same with a copy."

"That Cro-Magnon dude was pretty talented," Joe said.

"My brother, the art critic," Frank said, punching Joe playfully on the shoulder.

Sally led Frank and Joe from the central part of the mansion. "The east wing is now the Fossil Hall," she said.

The boys followed Sally into a large, spacious room with a high vaulted ceiling. A door at the far end was labeled Fossil Laboratory.

Evenly spaced around the floor were two dozen skeletons of prehistoric animals, ranging in size from a couple of feet to one that was almost twelve feet high and easily thirty feet long.

"Right now, we don't have the skeleton of anything larger than that Antrodemus over there in the center. It was a carnivorous dinosaur of the Jurassic period," Sally explained. "But we have actual-size models of some of the larger dinosaurs in our park outside. Oh, and over here, in this glass case we have an important piece. This is the fossil of an

6

Archaeopteryx—the supposed evolutionary link between the dinosaurs and the birds."

"What are these depressions in the floor?" Frank asked as he walked to the center of the hall. "They look as if they were made by some gigantic three-toed bird."

"This was one of Dr. Smith's ideas," Sally said. "These are reproductions of actual *Tyrannosaurus rex* footprints from a site in Texas. Do you see how they're spaced across the floor? The distance from one footprint to the next shows that this particular dinosaur could have run at speeds of up to twenty-five miles an hour."

"That's got me beat," Joe said.

"And check out their size," Frank said. "We could all sit down in one of these."

"In a few seconds, you'll see just how big they were," Sally said. "The footprints lead out the side door into the dinosaur park."

They followed the prints outside. A broad, green lawn was surrounded on three sides by the mansion and its wings. It stretched to a chain-link fence at the edge of the woods behind the museum. Rising from the shrubs and bushes were four full-size reproductions of some of the largest dinosaurs that ever existed. Two of the models were still surrounded by scaffolding.

"There it is, *Tyrannosaurus rex*," Joe said. "I'd recognize that monster anywhere. And the Apatosaurus we saw earlier. I know it used to be called a Brontosaurus. The other two are . . . Triceratops and Stegosaurus?"

"That's right," Sally said. "I see you know your dinosaurs."

"I read about them when I was a kid." Joe grinned. "Not half as much as you did, though."

Sally laughed. "Well, all those years of graduate school had to be good for something."

She stepped around a number of thick cables that snaked across the lawn to a small, modern-looking building on the far side of the park. A few construction workers stood near the structure.

"What's that?" Frank asked, following the line of the cables with his eyes.

"That's the control center," Sally said. "It coordinates the computers and controls for animating these 'Dinobots.'"

Joe blinked. "Dinobots?"

Sally smiled. "That's what our animation designer, Dan Parker, calls them."

"You mean these things are going to be able to move?" Joe said, his eyes lighting up.

"Well, sort of," Sally said. "At least enough to shake their heads and tails. But I did hear Dan say that one of them, the triceratops, may actually be able to walk back and forth. I don't think he's tested it yet."

"*That* I'd like to see," Joe enthused.

"You might get your chance," Sally said, looking up. "There's Dan now." A tall, red-haired man of about thirty was walking from the control shack. He wore jeans and an untucked denim shirt.

"Dan!" Sally called out.

Parker glanced up. A few long, quick strides brought him to Sally, Joe, and Frank.

"Meet Frank and Joe Hardy," Sally said, "friends of my family." She pointed a thumb toward the dinosaurs. "They're very interested in your Dinobots."

Parker shook their hands. "I just wish these babies were completely finished."

"They look pretty good," Sally said. "I hear the last scaffolding will come down tomorrow."

"But the mechanisms haven't been tested. I don't want any glitches. Scientists from all over the country will be here for our opening." Dan spoke in quick, animated bursts.

Sally nodded. "I'm nervous, too."

The young scientist ran a hand through his tangled red hair. "To top it off, my assistant Chuck quit yesterday for a higher-paying job somewhere else."

Joe glanced at Frank and raised his eyebrows. Frank knew what his brother was thinking. "Uh, Mr. Parker, we're not exactly dinosaur experts, but if you need some extra hands, Joe and I would be happy to pitch in," Frank said. "That is, if it's okay with you, Sally," he added.

"I'd appreciate any help." His smile suddenly turned to a frown. "Careful with that!" he yelled at the construction crew around the *Tyrannosaurus*

9

rex. "I'll catch you later," he told the Hardys and Sally. He rushed over to the Dinobot and began gesturing broadly.

"Thanks for the offer," Sally said to Frank and Joe. "But what about school?"

"Don't worry," Joe said. "We're out early tomorrow because of some teachers' meeting."

"And we've still got a free last period the other days," Frank added.

"Great," Sally said. "Let's check in with Dr. Smith, our director. I'm sure he'll be delighted to have some extra hands. Especially free ones!"

The boys followed Sally back to the administration wing. They went down a long hallway. Sally stopped in front of a door with a sign reading Clarence Smith, Director.

As she reached up to knock, a loud, angry-sounding male voice came from the office. It was answered by a quieter, but sharp, female voice.

"Um, maybe we should wait," Sally said. "I guess Dr. Smith is in conference."

Through the frosted glass window of the office door, Frank could make out a slim woman with bright red hair piled on top of her head. She was talking to a bald man seated behind a desk. Although their voices were low and he couldn't make out their words, it seemed to Frank that they were having some sort of disagreement.

Sally checked her watch. "My lunch hour is almost up, and I need to speak with our paleontologist, Carl Lubski. Would you both mind coming back to the Fossil Hall with me? By the time we return, Dr. Smith should be finished."

"Fine with me," Joe said.

Frank shrugged. "Let's go."

Sally led them back to the Fossil Hall, heading straight for the fossil lab in the back. Several large tables held collections of bones laid out in different configurations. In the corner, a man with long, gray-streaked hair huddled over a computer.

"Carl," Sally said. "I want you to meet Frank and Joe Hardy. They may be helping us."

Lubski grunted and waved his left hand, his eyes never leaving the computer. A diagram of a dinosaur rotated slowly on the screen.

"I know you're busy, Carl," Sally said, "but I have to talk to you."

Lubski nodded absently. "Let me finish what I'm working on," he said. "Just a moment more."

The trio wandered away from Lubski's desk, looking around the lab. Finally, the scientist switched off his computer and looked up, his glazed eyes seeming to refocus. "What is it you want to ask me?" he said.

"First, I'd like you to meet Frank and Joe Hardy," Sally said. "They've volunteered their services."

"Glad to meet you," Lubski said in a deep voice. To Joe he sounded very formal and serious. "What was your question, Sally?"

11

"I'm making up our final schedule," she said. "When do you expect to have the fossil collection ready for final publicity shots?"

Lubski sighed. "I'm doing my best to get it ready," he said. His eyes narrowed. "It didn't help that Parker crept in here last week and switched some of the name tags on my fossils."

"He's already apologized for his little joke," Sally said. "The tags didn't take long to switch back."

"But it wasted time! Which you, of all people, know we don't have. And I don't like practical jokes if that's what it was supposed to be."

"I know you're hard-pressed at the moment," Sally said diplomatically. "Frank and Joe might be able to help you."

"This is highly technical work," Lubski said. "It's not just a game of fossil jigsaw. I should be assisted by experienced graduate students."

"There must be some basic tasks that don't need high levels of expertise," Sally said.

"Maybe," Lubski said, rubbing his chin. "I'll let you know." He nodded goodbye, then marched from the fossil lab. *Not the most cheerful scientist,* Frank thought.

Sally shook her head. "It's bad enough being rushed without this feud between Lubski and Parker. Carl's a bit set in his ways. He doesn't always approve of Parker's methods." She sighed. "But Lubski is tops in his field, so we give him a certain leeway."

"Speaking of Parker," Joe said, "do you think he'd let us watch him test-run his dinosaurs?"

"Why not?" Sally checked her watch again. "But I really need to get back to work. Why don't you find Dan while I check in with Dr. Smith? Maybe he'll have time to meet you now."

Frank and Joe thanked Sally for the tour and headed back outside. Joe knocked at the door of the control shack. There was no answer, but the door swung open. The Hardys peered inside the empty building. A large window looked out over the dinosaur replicas, with a control panel stretching beneath it.

"Welcome to Dinobot Central," Frank said.

"I'd love to give this a try," Joe said, looking at the instrument panel eagerly.

"Out—now!" Frank half-dragged his brother away from temptation. Then he noticed a small wooden doorway leading from the main room of the control center.

"Mr. Parker?" Frank said, walking to the far side of the room.

The half-open door revealed a makeshift workshop. A large computer setup dominated a wooden table, surrounded by tangles of electronics gear. Scientific manuals were stacked on a shelf.

"Looks like Parker's workbench," Joe said.

"And I think I know what the work in progress is." Frank stepped into the small lab and picked up a pair of large goggles. They had an attachment in

13

front about the size and shape of a cigar box and were fastened to a helmet equipped with earphones. "It's a virtual reality setup—or at least the nuts and bolts of one."

Frank tapped the box. "Inside here are two tiny television screens, one for each eye," he explained. "Together they create a 3-D picture for the viewer. The scene should fill up the entire field of vision—three hundred and sixty degrees all around."

Joe's eyes twinkled. "Let's give it a try," he said, holding the goggles in front of him, ready to put them on.

Frank frowned. "I think we should wait for Parker."

"Just for a few seconds won't hurt," Joe said, slipping the goggles over his face.

"Are you sure you know what you're doing?" Frank asked his brother.

"It's easy," Joe said. "The wire from the back of the helmet leads to the computer console over there. All you have to do is hit the on switch."

"Here goes," Frank said, flicking the switch. A dull whirring sound filled the small office.

"Wow!" Joe burst out. "It's a prehistoric landscape." He sat quietly for several seconds, absorbed in the scene before his eyes. "This is so cool. I'm surrounded by giant ferns. Whoa, now there's a herd of dinosaurs eating some kind of horsetails. They kind of look like rhinoceroses."

"Probably Anchiceratops," Frank offered.

"Oh, and I see a Plateosaurus charging through

14

the underbrush behind me," Joe said, turning his head as if the prehistoric creatures were right behind him. "And there—"

Joe's narrative turned into a cry of pain. He grabbed his head, pushing at the goggles. Sparks suddenly showered from the computer console.

And Joe Hardy toppled to the lab floor!

2 A Surprising Threat

"Joe!" Frank yelled. He slammed the off button on the console and ran for his brother, who lay crumpled on the floor. Frank yanked the helmet off Joe and helped him to a sitting position.

Joe's eyes fluttered and he shook his head. He began to look around, his face pale.

"Wha—" he said groggily. "What was that?"

"Take a few deep breaths," Frank said. "Give your head a minute to clear."

Joe sat quietly for a moment and then looked up at Frank. "What happened?"

"I think you got zapped by a short circuit somewhere in the goggles," Frank said.

"Some zap," Joe said. "I thought I'd been hit by prehistoric lightning." He struggled to his feet with Frank's help.

16

"Obviously Parker hasn't perfected his system yet." Frank looked hard at the gear on the floor.

"Not yet," Joe agreed. "But he's really got something there. You should have seen it, Frank! For a moment I thought I could reach out and pat those critters."

"Well, he'll have to work the bugs out before anyone else uses it," Frank said. "The museum can't risk anyone being electrocuted."

"True," Joe said, "unless their idea of fun is getting knocked on the head with a hammer."

"What are you two doing in here?" a voice growled from the doorway. The Hardys spun to see Dan Parker. Sally stood behind him, poking her head into the workshop.

"Mr. Parker, I was—" Joe began.

"You were using my experimental goggles," Parker finished, glaring at the headgear on the floor. Then he noticed the cloud of blue smoke coiling around his computer console. "What happened?" he demanded. "Did you break it?"

"No," Joe said quickly. "Look, I'm sorry I used the helmet. We came in here looking for you and when I saw it, I couldn't resist. But when I tried it on, all I got was spark city."

"Oh, no!" Sally said. "Joe, are you okay?"

Joe nodded. Parker ran to the headgear, picked it up carefully, and began to inspect it. "It shorted out?" he asked. "You didn't tinker with anything, did you?"

"I just hit the on switch," Frank said. "It seemed like the computer malfunctioned."

"There was no one in here when you came in? And the door was open?" Parker said in a rush, as if he were trying to put a puzzle together.

"That's right," Frank replied. "As Joe said, we're sorry."

Parker waved a hand at him absently. "I don't want you sneaking around my office, but that's not what worries me. Someone has obviously been tampering with my equipment." He turned to Sally. "And we both can guess who that is, can't we?"

Sally sighed. "Dan, you don't know that."

A cold smile curved across Parker's face. "No, I don't. But Carl has made his attitude toward my work fairly clear."

Frank and Joe exchanged a quick look. Lubski and Parker certainly didn't hesitate to blame each other for their troubles. "The problem seemed to come from the computer," Frank said. "How could someone program a short circuit?"

"To program the virtual reality sequences—or tamper with them—you must disconnect the equipment. It's possible everything was reconnected incorrectly." Parker said. "I won't really know until I have a chance to inspect everything."

"So your think Lubski might be paying you back for switching his fossil labels?" Joe said.

Parker looked surprised. "You guys catch on quick. I'll just say it wouldn't surprise me."

18

"But he wouldn't really mess with this program, would he?" Joe said. "I mean, this is the cutting edge of technology. It's really cool."

"You and I might think so," Parker said. "But to Lubski this is a glorified video game."

"At any rate, we don't know that Carl has even been in here," Sally reminded him. "I hope it was just some computer malfunction. I wouldn't like to think that someone has been tampering with equipment."

"Okay, it may have just been an accident," Parker admitted. "It hasn't really been tested yet. Fortunately I have backup copies of the virtual reality program in my safe. And I'm the only one who knows the combination." He looked down at Frank and Joe. "When I check out everything, I'll happily give you a *supervised* demonstration."

"Thanks," Joe said. "We actually came in here to ask you if we could see the Dinobots in action. The door was open."

"No problem," Parker said. "But it will have to wait until I have some free time later this afternoon."

"Great," Frank said. "In the meantime, we promise we won't touch anything else."

"We're really sorry," Joe apologized again.

"Enough already," Parker said with a laugh. "I was planning to test the virtual reality goggles myself when I got back. Looks like Joe saved me a bit of a jolt."

Joe grinned. "Glad I could help."

"I still need to introduce you to Dr. Smith," Sally

19

said to Frank and Joe. "Why don't we see if he's free now?"

The boys agreed and turned to leave. "I hope we get a chance to help you with some of your exhibits," Joe said.

"Me, too," Parker said. He was already at the computer console, checking his equipment.

Frank and Joe walked with Sally across the dinosaur park.

"Sally, do *you* think Lubski would tamper with Parker's equipment?" Frank asked. "I mean, that shorted-out helmet could've really hurt someone."

"Yeah—like me," Joe pointed out.

"I don't know," Sally said. "Lubski was pretty angry about Parker's little joke. He doesn't hold Parker's work in very high regard. Still, I can't imagine him trying to harm anyone."

The three entered the administration wing and started down the hall. Shouting still resounded from behind Dr. Smith's door. From what Frank could see, though, the bald man was now alone in the office. "What do you mean there's no one by that name?" Frank heard through the door. "I was talking to her in person not more than half an hour ago."

Frank heard a telephone receiver being slammed down on its cradle. The door to Smith's office flew open, and a short man flew out. He stopped when he saw Frank, Joe, and Sally.

"What is it, Sally? I'm in a bit of a rush," Smith said.

"Dr. Smith, this is Frank Hardy and his brother, Joe," Sally said. "They're old friends of mine, and they've volunteered to help us get ready for the opening. How about it?"

"Great," Smith said, nodding quickly. "We can use as much help as we can get. Sally, you're in charge of breaking them in and showing them the ropes." The director seemed very distracted and kept fiddling with the pockets of his jacket. "Have you seen Lubski?"

"We talked to him a while ago in his lab. He left on some kind of errand but might be back there by now," Sally said.

"But you don't think he's in this wing?" Smith asked cautiously.

Sally looked puzzled. "I don't think so. We didn't see him on the way in."

"Ah." Smith's eyes nervously scanned the hall. "Well, I'm late for an appointment. Nice meeting both of you, and welcome aboard." Smith took off.

"Was it something we said?" Joe asked as the three watched the retreating figure.

"I don't know what's gotten into him." Sally frowned. "He's not usually so jumpy."

"Everybody around here seems a little jumpy," Frank said.

"Must be nerves over the grand opening, huh?" Joe added.

"I guess so," Sally said. "But I would have liked a

warmer welcome for you two. I hope it doesn't scare you off."

"Not a chance," Frank said. "That makes it all the more interesting. It'll be as much fun observing people as observing dinosaurs."

Sally smiled. "I forgot that detective blood runs in your family. Well, observe to your heart's content, Sherlock," she teased. "Scientists can be an odd lot."

The three walked through the offices, passing a number of employees, some of whom waved a hello to Sally. As they emerged into the bright afternoon sunlight, Frank saw a figure running toward them. It was Carl Lubski. The paleontologist stopped in front of them, and he was completely out of breath. "Is Smith . . . in his office?" he gasped.

"No. He just left for an appointment. We—" Sally started.

Lubski slammed a fist into his open palm. "That—" He was so angry, he bit off whatever he was going to say.

"What is it, Carl?" Sally said. "Can I help?"

Lubski wiped his forehead and shook his head angrily. "If only it were that easy." Frank was amazed to see what a temper the man had.

"You know," Lubski sputtered, "Elsa Mansfield had the right idea—to just disappear. Just stay as far away from this enterprise as possible. It's doomed!"

"What are you talking about, Carl?" Sally said.

22

But Lubski wasn't listening. His face was red and his breath came in short, harsh gusts. Then he turned his fury on Sally, Frank, and Joe.

"If things don't change around here, and I mean soon, then I guarantee you—this museum will never open!"

3 Heads Up!

His face still twisted in anger, Carl Lubski turned abruptly from Sally, Frank, and Joe and stormed off toward the Fossil Hall.

"What was that all about?" Frank asked.

"I wish I knew." Sally stared in shock after the paleontologist. "I never saw Carl so angry."

"Who's Elsa Mansfield?" Frank asked.

Sally turned back, shaking the shocked look from her face. "She's a scientist here at the museum—an expert on paleolithic art," she said. "You know, like the cave paintings done by Cro-Magnon people during the last Ice Age. Elsa is away at the moment on an expedition. I don't know why Lubski would call that 'disappearing.'"

"What does Lubski want changed around here?" Joe asked, wondering about the man's threat.

"That's one for you detectives," Sally said. "Maybe he's still mad at Parker."

Frank looked off toward the Fossil Hall. Sally was right: These scientists *were* an odd lot. But he wondered if there were more to Lubski's threat than a professional's eccentricity.

"So, what would you like us to do here this afternoon?" he asked, turning to Sally.

"Why don't we call it a day?" Sally said. "My nerves are shot. We can start fresh tomorrow."

"Sounds good," Joe said. "We just have a couple of classes, then we'll head over."

"Thanks," Sally said. "I'll see you then."

"The museum is more interesting than I had imagined," Frank said as he drove the Hardys' van home.

"I told you that you wouldn't be disappointed," Joe said. "Too bad Chet's been grounded. He'd love the place. I can't wait to see those Dinobots in action."

"I was actually thinking more about the present-day mysteries," Frank said.

"You think Lubski messed around with Parker's virtual reality stuff?" Joe said.

Frank shrugged. "I don't know. But if he did, why suddenly start making threats that the museum wouldn't open?"

"And how would he have any control over that anyway?" Joe noted.

Frank thought for a moment. "It's pretty obvious

25

that Dr. Smith wanted to avoid running into Lubski. And Lubski was mighty upset to hear that Smith had left. I wonder what's up with those two," he said, turning into their driveway.

"I don't know," Joe said. "But I have the feeling we're going to find out."

"I love it when we're on a case," Frank said with a grin.

Frank and Joe were up early the next morning. The breakfast table was a bit emptier than usual. Their aunt Gertrude was visiting an old friend in Arizona, and their father, Fenton Hardy, busy with an investigation, had already left. The boys knew that when he was in the middle of a case, it occupied almost all of his time—and his thoughts.

Laura Hardy was there, though, and during breakfast the boys filled their mother in on the work they would be doing at the museum. Then they headed to school. By midmorning, they were on their way back to the museum.

Joe parked the van in the back of the lot, leaving plenty of room for the construction workers and their materials. Several workmen were setting up a tall aluminum pole next to the front gate for a floodlight. Frank and Joe went to the administration wing in search of Sally. She was not in her office, so they headed over to the Hall of Prehistory.

"Have you seen Ms. Jenkins?" Frank asked one of the men working on the panoramic displays.

"In the far wing, I think," the man replied.

At the Fossil Hall, the boys found Sally talking to Carl Lubski as he stood by the large Antrodemus skeleton. Lubski's temper seemed to have returned to a more reasonable state.

As they approached, Sally was saying, "Thanks for putting in all the extra time on the fossil exhibit. That's a centerpiece of the museum."

"I agree—that's why I think it's worth it to get it done right," Lubski said.

Seeing the Hardys, Sally broke into a smile. "Hey!" she said brightly. "Ready to work?"

Joe pushed up the sleeves of his sweatshirt. "Point the way."

Lubski nodded at the boys. "I regret that scene yesterday," he apologized. His deep voice sounded sincere. "That's the bad part of working too hard—the slightest thing can set you off."

"No problem." Frank smiled. "Maybe we can help with some of that work."

"You took the words right out of my mouth," Sally said. She turned to Lubski. "I was planning to send Frank and Joe to you today."

"Fine," Lubski said. "There's enough to do that doesn't require an advanced degree."

"Great. I'll see all of you later," Sally said, turning away from the dinosaur skeleton.

When she had left, Lubski faced the boys. "I really am sorry about yesterday. Some of my colleagues just manage to get on my nerves."

"Like Dan Parker?" Frank ventured.

Lubski nodded. "Parker couldn't make it as a

27

true paleontologist. He left the field to play around with his . . . robots."

"The replicas are interesting, though," Joe pointed out. "They'll draw people to the museum."

"Showmanship instead of science," Lubski growled. "Parker has his precious Dinobots painted with all sorts of bright colors. Absurd!"

"Isn't it possible that—" Frank began.

"And the way he has distorted the implied bone structure," Lubski said, plowing on. "No reputable paleontologist would approve of that."

Frank shot a look at Joe. Clearly, Lubski's anger at Parker went beyond the practical jokes Parker played. Frank didn't want to see another blowup.

"So, how can we help you?" he asked quickly.

"The smaller fossils must be moved," Lubski said. "I'm rearranging them to make room for a large one I hope to complete before the opening."

"Sure," Joe said. "Which ones, and where do you want them?"

"Not so fast, young man. First, I need to tell you a little about fossils so that you'll know what you're doing."

"Fire away," Frank said. "I brought along a pad to take notes."

"Very good," Lubski said. "To start with, do you know what fossils are?"

"Bones of prehistoric animals?" Joe said, feeling as if he were in school but in a class he liked.

"More than that," Lubski said. "They are a wonder of nature." He gazed fondly at the skeletons as he spoke. "When a prehistoric animal died, it fell to the ground and was soon reduced to a skeleton. Most of those bones were lost. But sometimes, the skeleton was gradually covered with sediment. As the sediment got thicker and thicker, it finally compacted into rock. Minerals entered the encased bones and preserved them. Now, millions of years later, the rock has been worn away by erosion, exposing the fossilized bones."

"It's more complicated than I thought," Joe said.

Lubski nodded. As he lectured, the scientist seemed much more relaxed. "Here is the fossilized skeleton of a Hypsilophodon, a rather small dinosaur from the Cretaceous period. It resembles the kangaroo in size and other respects. The hind legs are much more developed than the smaller forelegs. Its teeth indicate that it was herbivorous—that is, a plant eater. When we display it, we have to consider whether it ran on all four legs or just the hind ones."

Talking paleontology, Lubski seemed to forget about Frank and Joe. "Uh, is this one you want moved?" Joe asked.

Lubski held up a hand. "Patience," he said. "You can't just pick up a carefully assembled skeleton and trundle it around like a piece of furniture. I'll show you how to do it properly. First we have to finish some work in the Hall of Prehistory." He snorted. "As if I don't have enough work, I've been stuck with Mansfield's job."

"She's the expert on paleolithic art, right?" Frank asked.

"She's an archeologist," Lubski said. "And she should be getting our prehistory exhibits together. Instead, she's off in India on a dig. She claims that the site is soon to be bulldozed for a road or something and she can't get away. I guess I can't blame her," Lubski said with a sigh. "I'd do the same thing."

"When you said she'd disappeared yesterday, I thought you meant she was staying away from the museum on purpose," Joe said.

Lubski shook his head. "I was just blowing off steam," he grunted. He marched quickly from the Fossil Hall. Joe shrugged as he and Frank trailed along to the Hall of Prehistory and the exhibit of early humans at the center of the hall.

A replica of a cave was still under construction, its inside walls partially covered with reproductions of prehistoric paintings. Several carefully sculpted figures of early men and women were grouped around a campfire. In front of the cave was the case containing the bison sculpture that Frank and Joe had seen the afternoon before. It was flanked by display cases filled with other artifacts of the cave dwellers.

"Prehistoric art isn't exactly my field of study," Lubski said, "but I know a bit about it. This bison sculpture is one of my favorite pieces from that period."

30

"It sure is something," Frank said, admiring the clay sculpture.

As they spoke, an older man with gray hair and thick glasses entered the hall.

"Oh, Tom," Lubski called to the man. "I want to introduce two new volunteers."

Tom walked over to Lubski, his head bent and his eyes glued to the floor.

"This is Tom Smedly, our head custodian," Lubski said. The custodian nodded nervously, wiping his hands on a bandanna from his pocket before shaking hands with Frank and Joe.

"Pleased to meet'cha." Smedly's eyes darted around, never meeting the boys'. He backed away quickly. "Well, I got some cleanup to do here."

Frank and Joe watched the custodian leave. "Smedly's not the most talkative guy," Lubski noted. "But I thought you should meet him, since you'll see him around a lot."

He turned to Frank. "Take some notes as we go," he said. "To begin with, the cave paintings in this exhibit need to be finished. Make a note to see if Michael Murray can do it." Frank remembered the graduate student when they had met on their tour. "And the stones around the campfire need to be rearranged to look a bit . . . cruder," Lubski went on.

Frank and Joe followed Lubski to the other exhibits of primitive people. One of them showed a human ancestor called *Australopithecus* on his knees making a stone chopper. Another showed a group of scavenging ape-men trying to drive a cheetah away from its kill with sticks.

Lubski continued to dictate notes to Frank as they went along, and Joe made some notes of his own as well. There was so much information that Frank was sure he'd never get it all down. He put his pad down momentarily to help as Lubski and Joe rearranged the stones around the campfire.

"That's about all for the prehistoric humans exhibit—at least for now," Lubski said. "Let's get back to the fossil collection." The three left the Hall of Prehistory.

Frank stopped at the doorway. "Hey, I left my notebook on top of the bison case. It'll just take a second to get. Go on ahead."

Frank ran back to the Hall of Prehistory, finding a tall wooden ladder set up over the bison case. Tom Smedly stood on the top rung, stretching to attach a large light fixture to the ceiling.

Frank grabbed his notebook and turned to leave. Suddenly, a dismayed cry rang through the hall. Frank glanced to the top of the ladder.

Smedly wobbled precariously on the top rung. In the next instant, the metal light fixture slipped from the custodian's hands.

As Frank stared, it plummeted straight down— directly at Frank's head.

4 Up in the Air

Frank ducked, going into a roll. As he flung himself away, he caught a flash of movement. Then came a shattering crash, mere inches away. Frank tucked his head under his arms to escape flying glass fragments.

His heart thudding, Frank slowly looked around. The light fixture lay smashed on the floor. It had barely missed the bison case, smashing instead into the case next to it. Jagged glass splinters were everywhere.

As the sound of breaking glass subsided, Frank heard Smedly's voice. "Oh, no—oh, no!" Frank looked up to see the custodian scrambling down the ladder. "Are you all right?" the older man cried nervously.

Frank managed a shaky grin. "You missed me," he said as he rose to his knees.

Smedly's face was ashen as he steadied Frank. "I—I—" The man could barely speak. "The fixture just slipped out of my hand. It's kinda hard to hold with one hand while you try to attach it with the other. It was an accident."

By that time, other workers in that section of the hall had run over to Frank, joined by Joe and Carl Lubski. Joe stepped over the broken glass to help his brother to his feet.

"Careful," Frank said. "I've got bits of glass all over me." He went to brush himself off and nearly fell, still wobbly after the near miss.

"Oh, my goodness!" Sally ran into the hall, her eyes growing wider as she saw the shattered glass. "What on earth happened here?"

"I didn't mean to do it!" Smedly babbled.

"Do what?" Sally asked.

"Mr. Smedly had a little accident," Frank said. "A light fixture slipped from his hand—from the top of the ladder directly over my head."

"Oh, no!" Sally exclaimed. "It didn't hit you, did it?"

Frank shook his head. "I managed to get out of the way."

"I—I'll clean it up right away," Smedly said. "Let me get my broom."

Frank carefully picked pieces of glass from his clothes.

"Good thing you're fast on your feet, huh, bro?"

Joe said, kicking away some of the bigger pieces of glass from where they were standing.

"And it's a good thing this fixture missed the bison case," Lubski put in. "Can you imagine if it had crashed through, hitting the sculpture? We'd have a real tragedy on our hands."

Sally put a hand to her chest. "Don't even *think* about it," she said. "I'm just glad you weren't hurt, Frank." Everyone looked up as Smedly returned with a broom and a dustpan. The custodian's hands still shook as he began sweeping. He kept his eyes to the floor.

"Smedly, why were you trying to put up that heavy fixture by yourself?" Sally scolded. "That's an accident waiting to happen."

"I—I thought I could do it," Smedly said. His face was pained as if every word were an agonizing effort. "I've done it before."

"Well, you'll have to tell that to Dr. Smith," Sally said. "I'm not explaining this to him by myself. Come on—we're going to his office." Frank could see that Sally looked as shaken as Smedly. The custodian's eyes were wide with fright as he followed Sally through the broken glass and out of the hall.

Lubski sighed. "Looks like we'll need a new plan. Sorting through this mess will have to be your first job," he told Frank and Joe. "Pick all the stone tools out of the broken glass. Just line them up on the floor here and we'll sort through them later."

Lubski picked up a stone chopper, a fist-sized

35

rock that had been fractured by an early human to create a sharp edge. He carried it to a clear area of the floor and set it down carefully. Frank and Joe followed his example, carrying other stone tools and arrowheads to the side. Bits of glass crunched under their feet as they moved.

After a few minutes, Lubski said, "It seems you've got the idea. Keep going while I see about a new display case in the storeroom."

Frank and Joe spent an hour separating the prehistoric tools from the broken glass, lining up the artifacts on the floor.

Sally came back as they were finishing. "Thanks a lot," she said. "You're doing a great job. How about a lunch break?"

"Sounds good," Joe said. "Is there someplace around here we can get some food?"

"There's a diner a mile or so back in Sackville Corners," Sally said. "I'd go with you, but lately I've just been grabbing a quick bite at my desk. When you get back, maybe you can help Parker for a while."

"We're not going to help Lubski move his fossils?" Joe asked.

"I just spoke to Lubski," Sally said. "He has to go to Bayport to get a replacement case made. In the meantime, I'm sure Parker can use you."

"Fine with me," Joe said. "I've been hoping to get a closer look at his equipment."

"Good. I'll meet you back here after lunch," Sally said. *"Bon appetit!"*

A few minutes later, Joe was pulling the van up to a small diner in Sackville Corners. It was the largest building at the intersection that made up most of the small town. A gas station, a grocery, and a hardware store stood on the other three corners.

The boys entered, grabbed a booth next to the front window, and ordered burgers from the waitress. Joe leaned back in the vinyl seat. "You're not sitting on any glass, are you?"

Frank half smiled. "I think I got it all off me. But I'm afraid Smedly will be sweeping up glass for the rest of the afternoon. Poor guy—he looked terrified when Sally marched him off to Smith's office."

"You can't blame them for getting upset," Joe said. "Think about it—they've had disasters around two of the museum's star attractions, the bison sculpture and Parker's high-tech stuff."

Frank looked at his brother closely. "Are you saying you think there's some kind of connection? And that Smedly might have been *aiming* for the bison case?"

Joe shrugged. "I was just thinking of the look on Lubski's face when he saw how close the fixture had come to the bison. If you wanted to get at Lubski, that would be a sure way to do it."

"But Smedly?" Frank said skeptically. "He was terrified when that thing fell. And he really seemed concerned that I was okay. I wonder why somebody would want to get at Lubski anyway."

"If Parker thinks Lubski is the one who messed

with his virtual reality equipment, he could be looking to get back at him," Joe offered.

"That's one if and one maybe," Frank pointed out. "There's no question that everyone at the museum seems pretty edgy. But for all we know, they're that way all the time."

Joe shrugged. "Maybe we should ask Sally what *she* thinks."

"Good idea. Let's ask her over for dinner," Frank suggested. "That'll give us more time to talk." The waitress placed down plates of burgers and fries. "I'll call Mom when we're done eating." He watched Joe attack his burger. "In your case, that should be in about five minutes."

When they got back to the museum, Frank parked in the back of the lot again. Heading for the administrative wing, Frank saw Sally and Smedly talking outside. Sally waved them over.

"Hi," Sally said. "I was just telling Tom that if he has a job to do that takes more than one person, he can call on the two of you. He shouldn't try to do everything singlehandedly. You don't mind, do you?"

"Not at all." Frank turned to Smedly. "We'll be around all afternoon if you need us."

"Thanks," Smedly said, his face reddening. "I'll remember what you said," he told Sally. With that, he took off for the Hall of Prehistory.

"So how was lunch?" Sally asked.

"Not bad," Joe said. "We're all set to go again. Should we head over to help Dan Parker?"

Sally nodded. "He's about to test the moves on one of the Dinobots. You'll find him in the dinosaur park making final adjustments."

"We're on our way," Joe said eagerly.

"I'll join you," Sally said. "I'd like to see how Dan's coming along, too."

They cut through the administrative wing to come out onto the central lawn area, where the dinosaur park was located. Entering the park from this side, instead of from the Hall of Prehistory, Frank noticed that the trees and shrubs had been carefully planted to blend into the wooded area behind the park and yet still allow for walkways and clear views of the dinosaurs.

At the center of the area, Parker was busily examining cables for the huge dinosaur models. He grinned when he saw Sally and the boys and signaled them over. "This has been a rough day," Parker said. "There are so many things to check. I could really use some help."

"Looks as if you got here just in time," Sally told Frank and Joe. "I'm going to wander around a little, but I'll catch up with you later." She headed off down one of the pathways as Frank and Joe turned their attention to Parker.

"I think the exhibit is almost ready," Parker said. "But I have to double-check every part. I have a lot riding on these big guys."

"The models are actually going to move?" Joe asked, craning his neck to stare up at the huge dinosaur models around them.

"Limited movement." Parker took off his baseball cap and wiped the sweat from his forehead. "Their eyes will move left and right, the heads can turn, the mouths open and close, and the tails move back and forth."

"But they stay in place while those parts are moving, right?" Frank said.

"Not all of them," Parker said, his face lighting up. "I'm working on an advanced model that may actually be able to move back and forth. It's this one here—the horned dinosaur, Triceratops. It has a small control chamber inside with an access door underneath."

"So it could actually roam around the park?" Joe said, looking around the wooded area.

"Won't that be dangerous for museum visitors?" Frank asked.

"Well, it won't roam far," Parker said. "There'll be a waist-high fence along the path over there." He pointed to the walkway that led from the Fossil Hall to the control shack. "The public will stand behind it. We don't want our Dinobots accidentally squishing the paying customers," he said with a boyish grin.

"Can any of the other Dinobots be controlled that way?" Joe asked.

"The Triceratops is the only one operated independently. The others will be run from the control shack. Their movements are preprogrammed by a computer, but they can also be operated with a joystick on the control panel. I'll show you."

Frank and Joe followed him, stepping over the many cables laid across the ground from the Dinobots to the control shack. "These cables will all be buried underground before the opening," Parker noted.

"How does the animation actually work?" Frank asked as they went in.

"It's done by a combination of mechanical linkages and pneumatic air valves attached to an air compressor here in the shack. Manual control runs through a microprocessor controlled by the joystick."

"Sort of like a video game," Joe said.

"Exactly," Parker said.

"Is there an emergency shut-off switch?" Frank asked. "In case things get out of hand."

"Oh, sure," Parker said. "Right here on the control panel." He pointed to a red button. "The dinos are just machines, but any machines their size can be dangerous.

"We'll run the preprogrammed motions first," Parker continued, standing in front of the control panel and looking through the large window that faced the dinosaur park. "Power on!" he said, flipping a switch.

A faint hum came from the computer, and somewhere under the control panel came the whirring sound of an air compressor. Frank and Joe watched through the window as the Tyrannosaurus began to move its head and tail. At the same time, it gave out a very convincing roar.

"That's funny," Parker said. "The Apatosaurus isn't moving. It's also supposed to lower its head and open its mouth. Joe, would you mind seeing if the cable connection is loose? It's just in front of the Apatosaurus."

Joe ran out of the shack and over to the jumble of cables in front of the dinosaur model.

"There are too many connections," Joe called back. "I can't tell which is the right one."

"Hold on." Parker headed for the door. "I think I know which one."

He ran over to Joe and rooted through the cables, picking up one to twist the connection. Suddenly, the head and long neck of the Apatosaurus swung down and it began opening and closing its mechanical jaws. "Wow," Frank said under his breath. It really did look lifelike. He went outside for a closer look.

"Looking good," Frank called out as he approached Parker. Parker turned and gave Frank a thumbs-up sign. Just then, the neck of the Apatosaurus swept down, and Frank gasped. The huge head knocked Parker off his feet with a violent blow. Then its jaws opened and closed again, gripping Joe around the waist in a firm, quick motion.

As Joe let out a surprised cry, waving his arms and legs around frantically, the massive dinosaur lifted him high up into the air!

5 Danger: Triceratops Crossing

"Yeow!" Joe yelled. "What the—?" He beat his fists against the dino-jaws clamped around his waist.

Frank stared in horror as the mechanical Apatosaurus swept Joe high into the air. Joe looked like an tiny mouse about to be swallowed by a giant cat. Frank saw that Parker was still on the ground. Without a second thought, Frank raced inside the control shack.

Frank reached for the emergency off button on the control panel, then hesitated. What if killing the power made the dinosaur freeze in its original position, jaws open? Joe would be dumped forty feet to the ground.

But what choice did he have? Frank hit the red

44

button. Instantly, the dinosaur models stopped. The Apatosaurus froze, its jaws still around Joe. Frank let out a sigh of relief. Then he ran back outside.

He sprinted over to Parker. The scientist sat on the ground, holding his head in his hands. He was obviously still dazed from the blow he'd gotten from the Dinobot.

"Frank! Get me down from here!" Joe shouted above him.

"Don't panic!" Frank called back. "We'll get things under control in a flash." He bent back down to Parker. "The Apatosaurus grabbed Joe. How do we get him down?"

Parker lifted up a pale face, squinting in pain as he stared at the mechanical dinosaur. "Oh, no!" he exclaimed. "Help me back to the control shack."

Frank helped Parker to his feet and guided the groggy man to the controls. Parker slumped in the chair in front of the console and held his head, struggling to concentrate.

"Turn on the power, then press the button labeled Apatosaurus." Parker kept his eyes closed, breathing in shallow gasps. "Ease the joystick forward to lower the head to the ground, and then press the button labeled Jaws Open."

Frank nodded, completely focused on the control panel. He turned the power back on and then grabbed the joystick. The control was very sensitive. Even though he moved it carefully, the Apatosaurus head swung in an arc, nearly bashing

45

Joe into the ground. Frank immediately eased the stick back. The Dinobot head with Joe went sailing up into the air again.

"Take it easy!" Joe hollered. Frank winced as he saw Joe's body being jerked around.

"Push the joystick forward *very* gently," Parker said.

This time Frank managed to inch the head down slowly closer and closer to the grass. Afraid to get too close, Frank pressed the Jaws Open button a second too soon. The huge jaws gaped and Joe dropped the last six feet, flopping onto the ground.

Frank turned off the power as Parker sighed in relief. Then he rushed outside to Joe, who was staggering to his feet.

"Whoa! That's a new one for me," Joe said. "Never thought I'd be an afternoon snack for a dinosaur." He brushed grass from his clothes as he steadied himself. He yelped with pain when he put his full weight on his foot.

"Sorry about that last drop," Frank said. "I need a little more practice on the controls."

"No kidding—but you'll have to practice on somebody else," Joe said. "I've had enough."

The Hardys looked up to see Dan Parker walking slowly toward them. The tall man still looked pale but was a little less wobbly. "Are you okay, Joe?" he said.

"I think so," Joe said. "But what happened?"

Parker shook his head, his eyes scanning the mass

of cables at their feet. He picked up the cable he had tightened just before the accident. "I think this cable was loosened on purpose," he said, turning it over in his hand. "As bait."

"Are you saying this wasn't just a simple malfunction?" Frank said. "I mean, this machine was meant to grab Joe?"

Parker nodded. "You have to program every move the machine makes. Whoever loosened the cable probably reprogrammed the Dinobot to grab whoever tightened it."

"Can the Apatosaurus be programmed to do something like that?" Joe asked.

"Sure," Parker said. "The machine can make each of those moves. It's no big deal to change the program so the old boy did them in sequence."

"And for a couple of minutes the Dinobots were on, and no one was in the control shack," Frank reminded them. "Someone could have preprogrammed some of the moves and then slipped inside just long enough to make the Apatosaurus grab Joe."

The young Hardy gazed at the huge Dinobot. "I was kind of hoping it was an accident."

"No way," Parker said. "I programmed the Dinobots myself. I would hardly program one of them to grab somebody like that." He looked at Frank and Joe and raised an eyebrow. "But I have an idea who might."

"Carl Lubski?" Frank and Joe said together.

Parker nodded and looked away, deep in thought. "That guy would do anything to discredit me," he mumbled.

"There's a difference between doing that and seriously hurting you," Frank said.

Parker shrugged. "He could also be trying to get Smith to believe that this exhibit is too dangerous for the public."

Joe looked up at the open jaws of the Apatosaurus just above him. "Well, it does seem a bit dangerous," Joe said.

"As I said, the public will be kept well back behind a fence," Parker said defensively. "The fence will be put up before the museum opens."

Suddenly, Sally and Tom Smedly ran up to the Apatosaurus from different footpaths. "I heard yelling," Sally said. "Is everything okay?"

"Just working out a kink in the Dinobots," Joe said casually, shooting Frank a look.

Frank got the message. Joe didn't want to worry Sally or get Parker in trouble. He wanted to see the Dinobot exhibition open on time.

"Then why were you shouting like that? And why are you hopping around on one foot?" Sally asked.

"Uh, well, I twisted my ankle a bit when I fell," Joe admitted.

"You fell? From where?" Sally said.

"One of the Dinobots was misprogrammed and I got a bit . . . tangled up with it," Joe said carefully.

"It wasn't me," Smedly blurted out. "I was in the administration wing helping Dr. Smith."

48

Sally gave him a baffled look. "No one is accusing you, Tom."

"Well, I—I'm just making sure." The custodian turned away from the group and headed back down the footpath. "Seems like I always get blamed for everything," he mumbled.

Sally turned back to Parker. "Is there a problem with the Dinobots I should know about?" she asked firmly.

Parker hesitated. "As I said, I'm double-checking all the programs. There's no danger to the public. Any problems I have will be ironed out by the time we open."

"I hope so," Sally said. "Look, it's about time to call it a day anyway. Joe, will you be able to make it to your van with that ankle?"

"No problem," Joe said. "It feels better already."

Sally turned to leave, and Parker slapped Joe on the back. "Thanks again for your help," he said.

"Are you all right?" Frank asked.

The scientist nodded. "A good night's sleep will help. See you tomorrow."

Frank and Joe caught up to Sally, and Frank asked her over to dinner. "I know Mom would love to see you again," he added.

"That sounds great," Sally said. "What time?"

"About seven-thirty?" Frank said.

"See you then," Sally said.

Sally arrived promptly at seven-thirty to a warm greeting from Laura Hardy. "Gertrude is away, and

49

Fenton just called—another late night on his investigation."

"Dad taught me all about them," Sally said.

"Dinner is just about ready," Mrs. Hardy said. "While I check on the pasta, there are cheese and crackers in the living room."

Frank, Joe, and Sally settled themselves in the large, comfortable living room. "How's the ankle?" Sally asked.

"Oh, it'll be fine," Joe said. "Just a little bit tender. I won't even feel it by tomorrow."

"I'm glad you weren't seriously injured," Sally said. "I'm sorry about everything that's been happening. The two of you are getting pretty beat up as volunteers."

"Parker claims that someone tampered with the computer program and made the accident happen," Frank said. "What do you think?"

Sally smiled ruefully. "Don't tell me—he thinks Lubski is that someone, right? The two of them are like cats and dogs." She sighed. "But I've got to think of it as an accident at this point."

"A lot of 'accidents' seem to be happening at the museum," Joe pointed out.

"I know." Sally frowned unhappily. "But let's suppose that Lubski did what you say. If he were caught, there goes his whole career. Carl takes his science too seriously for that. He might pull a practical joke to pay Parker back for his prank, but I can't see him going farther."

"What if Parker set up the accident himself to make Lubski look bad?" Frank mused.

Sally stared. "Why would he do that?"

"So that Smith would fire Lubski, which would mean Parker could do his work in peace," Frank said.

Joe shook his head. "All this because they disagree about approaches to take at the museum?"

"Well, it goes a bit deeper than that," Sally said. "Smith told me that Parker and Lubski have competed in the past for grants and positions. Lubski even wrote a scathing critique of Parker's methods and ideas in one of the professional journals. After that, Parker quit basic research and began working with animated dinosaurs."

"So Lubski plays a little rough, huh?" Joe said.

"So does Parker, in spite of his nice-guy ways," Sally said. "He's competed with Lubski to get a lot of the museum's funds for his Dinobot project."

"And he could get even more with Lubski out of the picture," Frank pointed out.

Sally shook her head wearily, then looked at the brothers. "I don't know what's going on. But I'm glad you're here to help. And if you can figure out a way to stop these accidents before they happen, I'd really appreciate it."

Mrs. Hardy came into the living room. "I hope you're hungry," she said. "The pasta's ready, and there's a lot of it."

Frank got up and put his arm around his mother.

"Don't worry, Mom. Have you ever known a time when we weren't hungry?"

Mrs. Hardy rolled her eyes. "I was talking to Sally," she said. "Try to leave some for her, will you?" she teased.

The four of them sat down to salad, pasta with marinara sauce, and fresh bread. After some hearty eating, dessert, and stories about the Hardys' investigations and Sally's graduate school adventures, Sally got up to leave.

"Thanks again," she told Mrs. Hardy. "The food and the company were wonderful."

Laura Hardy smiled. "I hope you'll be able to come by more often," she said.

"Me, too," Sally said. "Maybe when the museum finally opens and I can live a more normal life."

Frank and Joe walked Sally to her car in the driveway. "I may not be at the museum when you get there tomorrow. I've got building permits to renew in Bayport. You two check in with Parker to see if he still needs help—and let's see if we can make it through a day disaster-free," she added.

After school the next day, Frank and Joe drove back to the museum. They headed straight to the control shack to find Dan Parker.

"You're just in time," Parker said. Frank noticed that the scientist seemed fully recovered from his blow the day before. In fact, he looked as excited as a boy with a new toy. "I'm about to test the mother of all Dinobots. You won't believe what you're about to see. The Triceratops will actually walk back and forth."

"Great," Joe said. "What can we do to help?"

"I need two observers, one on each side of the dinosaur park," Parker said. "Take notes on how dinosaur movements look. We'll also discuss the safest route for the Dinobot."

"I'll stand by the Fossil Hall entrance," Frank said.

"And I'll go to the edge of the woods, near the control shack," Joe said.

"Good. Now the main thing is to be careful. Don't get close to the Triceratops. You remember what happened yesterday," Parker said with a wry grin. "Now I need you to help me climb into the Dinobot. I'll be operating it from a small cockpit inside."

"You mentioned that," Joe said. "I'm looking forward to seeing how this works."

"I have a small television camera in one of the eyes of the Triceratops and a small screen in the cockpit," Parker explained. "So I'll see about what the dinosaur would see, but only on one side. That doesn't give me much visibility. I also have a miniature version of the control panel and joystick that are in the shack."

He turned to Frank. "You take this handset for the radio intercom. I've got headphones in the Dinobot. That way, we'll stay in contact."

The three headed over to the Triceratops. Parker opened a trapdoor in the belly of the Dinobot. It

53

was only a few feet off the ground but very difficult to get through. Frank and Joe helped him squeeze into the small compartment.

"Good luck," Frank said as Parker closed the trapdoor. He and Joe started toward their observation posts. Frank's radio crackled to life. He could just make out what Parker was saying.

"I'm starting the motor now," Parker's staticky voice said.

Frank heard a low, rumbling sound from inside the Dinobot. "Wow, it's really cramped in here," Frank heard Parker mutter. "We'll take a step forward now. Frank, can you hear me?"

"Loud and clear," Frank said.

Frank watched as the huge right front leg of the Triceratops lifted. Then the right leg came down and the left one jerked up. The rear legs tried to follow in succession. The Dinobot lurched forward awkwardly.

"How does it look?" Parker asked from inside the Dinobot.

"Not too bad," Frank said. "But I don't think the hind legs are coordinated with the front ones."

"I was afraid of that," Parker sighed. "I'll have to adjust them later. Now I'm going to try shifting the Dinobot slightly to the right," Parker's scratchy voice said. "Make sure you stand well back. You're out of my line of vision on this small screen."

"Okay," Frank said. He stepped back as the Dinobot began pulling slowly into a turn.

Suddenly, Frank caught a slight movement from

the corner of his eye. Carl Lubski emerged from the Fossil Hall wing. His head was buried in a sheaf of papers as he set off across the dinosaur park. He seemed to be heading for the service building behind the control shack.

Frank turned back to the Triceratops. His eyes grew wide. The lumbering machine swung right into Lubski's path. And the paleontologist, lost in his reading, hadn't noticed the dinosaur.

"Parker, stop the Dinobot!" Frank shouted into the radio.

The radio only crackled with static. Frank looked up. The Triceratops lurched forward again. The scientist would be stomped flat!

6 A Disappearing Dinosaur

"Lubski! Watch out!" Frank shouted.

But the paleontologist didn't even hear the rumbling of the Dinobot. As the dinosaur lifted its heavy leg, Frank sprinted to Lubski, catching him in a leaping tackle at the last minute.

"What do you think you're—" Lubski yelled. He tumbled to the ground with Frank on top of him. His papers scattered as a huge dinosaur foot came stomping down inches from his body.

Rolling off Lubski, Frank looked up to see the Triceratops lumbering away, the low rumbling sound growing fainter as it moved. Frank stood up and put out a hand to help Lubski. "Sorry about that," he said. "Are you all right?"

The paleontologist stared after the mechanical dinosaur, his expression a mixture of fright and anger. "What on earth is going on?" Lubski's deep voice sputtered.

Frank helped Lubski to his feet. "Parker's testing the Dinobots," he said. He picked up the radio set he'd dropped. "Parker, do you hear me?"

The loud crackling died momentarily. "Yeah. How does it look?" Parker's staticky voice said.

Frank caught a glimpse of Lubski's red, scowling face. "Uh, you'd better stop. You almost stepped on someone," Frank said.

"What?" Parker's voice barked over the radio. There was a hesitation, then he said, "Okay, give me a second."

The Dinobot jerked to a stop, and the low throbbing sound suddenly died as Parker cut the power. Beside Frank, Lubski glared, muttering, "Some hotshot machinery . . . completely out of control."

Parker slid out through the trapdoor and hurried over.

"What kind of stunt was that?" Lubski burst out. "You could have killed me!"

Parker's jaw dropped, then came jutting up. "What were you doing walking in front of a moving machine? I'd call that a *dumb* stunt!"

As the argument warmed up, Joe arrived. "Hey, why'd you stop? I thought—"

"You have no right experimenting with these dangerous machines without notifying all personnel," Lubski said, interrupting Joe. "Or were you hoping to get rid of me the easy way?"

"Hardly, even though that'd make things easier for everyone," Parker sneered.

Lubski's face grew so red that Frank feared he might explode. Suddenly the scientist grabbed the radio from Frank's hand and threw it to the ground. "This isn't a game, Parker!" he roared.

Parker stared in fury at the older man. "You want to play games?" he demanded. "Do you see me throwing your stupid bones around?" He looked around wildly and finally scooped up some of Lubski's papers and threw them up to scatter in the air. Joe shot a look at Frank, and Frank shook his head, not knowing what to think.

"Why, you——" Lubski sputtered, taking a step toward Parker.

"Parker! Lubski! What's going on here?" a sharp voice cut in. Clarence Smith strode out of the Fossil Hall. The director looked from Parker to Lubski, his forehead creased in a scowl. "Can we try to act like adults here?"

Lubski still glared angrily. "Parker's running wild with his overgrown toys," he said, stabbing a finger at the Triceratops. "He almost killed me with that . . . thing. If Frank hadn't been here, I'd have been crushed."

Parker thrust his red face forward. "Not if you'd kept to the walkways, the way you're supposed to," he countered.

"Will somebody please tell me what's going on here?" Smith said, obviously losing patience with the feuding scientists.

58

"We were testing one of the Dinobots, and as Mr. Parker went into a turn, Mr. Lubski stepped into the machine's path," Frank said. "I thought he might have heard the dinosaur, but when he didn't, I pushed him out of the way."

"Did the Dinobot malfunction?" Smith asked in a worried voice.

Parker shook his head quickly. "No, it turned quite well."

Smith nodded. "Let's just settle this. Parker, post some warning signs when you're conducting a test. And Lubski, stick to the paths." He held up his hands before either man could argue. "Now can we get back to work? I don't have to remind you how much we have to do."

The director bent down to pick up Lubski's papers, and Frank and Joe rushed to help him. Frank could hear Lubski's angry snorting above him and got ready for another outburst. But Smith quickly handed the paleontologist his papers and began leading him back to the Fossil Hall. "Why don't you take the rest of the day off, Carl?" Smith said. "I think you've been working too hard."

"My work is what this place needs—solid scholarship," Lubski growled. "Not a lot of mechanical toys."

As they left, Parker sighed and turned to the boys. "Are you all right?" he asked Frank.

Frank nodded. "I'm just glad I got there in time. Lubski was so involved in his reading, he didn't even see you coming."

"It was quick thinking on your part." Parker shook his head. "I hate these stupid squabbles. But Lubski just brings out the worst in me."

"There wasn't any problem with the triceratops, was there?" Joe said. "From my angle, everything looked great. The movements were slow but pretty realistic."

"No, I got it going well," Parker said. "But this does make me a little worried. If Lubski can wander off the paths, then a visitor can. Even with fences up, there's always someone who wants to make his own rules."

"What about posting guards?" Frank suggested.

Parker frowned. "That's not a bad idea. Smith will never hire extra personnel—we're already over budget. But maybe we could relocate a couple of the museum guards." He thought for a moment. "You know, I'm going to run that by Smith. It might make him a bit less worried about the Dinobot exhibition."

Parker started toward the Fossil Hall, then turned. "Thanks again for your help," he called as he left the park.

Joe picked up the radio Lubski had smashed. "Looks like our mild-mannered scientists have a wild side," he said. "Could Parker have seen Lubski from inside the dinosaur?"

"I don't think so," Frank said. "He was turning at a pretty sharp angle. I'd say Lubski crossed just at the wrong moment."

"What about Lubski? Do you think he walked in front of the machine on purpose, so Smith would think the Dinobots are dangerous?" Joe suggested.

"He looked completely shocked to be in the path of an oncoming Triceratops." Frank frowned toward the fossil lab. "But he would love to see the plug pulled on Parker's dinos. We should find out more about Lubski and the museum. Why don't we take a look around the fossil lab while he's gone for the afternoon?"

"Do you think he might have something to do with the other accidents around here?" Joe asked.

"Not necessarily," Frank replied. "But it wouldn't hurt to know just what kind of work he's involved in."

"Let's go," Joe said. They cut across the dinosaur park to the back of the Fossil Hall. When they reached the door of Lubski's lab, Frank dug out a small lock-picking tool from his pocket. Joe tried the doorknob on the gray metal door. It turned easily.

"I guess Lubski left in such a hurry he didn't bother to lock up," Joe said.

"He even left his computer screen on," Frank noted as they slipped inside, closing the door behind them. The computer sat on a cluttered desk in front of a well-worn padded chair. Bookshelves lined the small office, and a metal filing cabinet was jammed into a corner.

Frank went straight to the desk, which was covered with stacks of scientific journals and computer magazines. Next to the computer was a pile of diskettes, which Frank quickly flipped through. They were all carefully labeled except for one, which he held up for Joe.

"Looks like Lubski keeps up with the latest computer technology," Frank said. "So he might have the expertise to reprogram the Dinobot—and sabotage the virtual reality program, too."

"Let's see what he's working on now," Joe sat down at the keyboard and scrolled the document on the screen up and down. "It's a paper about the K/T boundary. I remember reading about that. It's between the Cretaceous and the Tertiary periods, sixty-five million years ago."

"Right, when the dinosaurs disappeared," Frank said.

Joe nodded. "Many scientists believe that a comet or an asteroid hit the earth, setting off a chain of events that led to the sudden extinction of the dinosaurs. Others think the comet created a dense cloud of dust around the whole planet, blocking out the sunlight for months."

"And as the plant life died, so did the dinosaurs who ate them," Frank finished.

"Looks like Lubski is challenging both theories," Joe said, reading from the screen. "This article is titled '100,000 Years—That's Sudden?' He's saying that from the paleontological evidence, it seems that the dinosaurs gradually died out over a period of thousands of years."

"I bet Parker backs the killer-comet theory," Frank said. "Maybe that's where this feud began."

"Maybe," Joe said. "Let's see what's on this unlabeled disc." He switched the discs and tried to bring the new one up on the screen. "Ah-ha," he said, "this one needs a code word for access."

Frank raised his eyebrows. "So maybe Lubski *does* have something to hide."

"Or it could just be personal documents or financial records he wants to keep private," Joe said. "I'll put the original disc back in."

Frank nodded and looked around the office. "I don't see much else in here. Dr. Smith is right; it looks like Lubski works pretty hard." Joe stood up and Frank nodded toward the door. "Let's go back out through the Fossil Hall. That way, if anyone sees us, it will just look as though we've been working in there."

The boys left the lab, coming into the empty main hall. Most of the workers seemed to have gone home, and the skeletons rose silently from their fixed positions in the center of the room. Frank and Joe began to weave their way around them when Frank stopped suddenly.

"What is it?" Joe said.

Frank looked around, his forehead furrowed in thought. "I don't know. Do you see anything odd here, like maybe there's something missing?"

Joe turned in a watchful circle. "One of the fossils?"

"I don't think—" Frank murmured. He wandered over to the side of the hall nearest the dinosaur park. A large glass display case stood against the wall. Joe joined him.

"Place looks about the same to me," Joe said.

Frank shook his head. "No. Weren't there two cases here? Where's the one with that small fossil Lubski was so excited about? It was the only fossil in the hall in a display case—some kind of bird or something."

"Oh, yeah," Joe said. He whirled around. "It should around here somewhere."

"The Archaeopteryx, the protobird," Frank said suddenly, snapping his fingers. "That's the name. I've got it written down in my notebook."

A few feet away, Joe dropped to one knee. "Check this out," he said. "See the indentations on the floor tiles? It looks like a square case used to sit here."

"I knew it," Frank said. He looked around. "Maybe it got moved." The two boys made a sweep of the hall, carefully checking the cases pushed against the walls as well as a large one almost in the middle of the room.

"It's not here," Joe said finally.

"So where'd it go? I didn't see it in the fossil lab," Frank said.

Joe stepped over to a small door next to the entrance to the fossil lab. He glanced over at Frank, who shrugged. "Some kind of closet?" Frank guessed. Joe pulled open the door and they both peered inside the small dark room.

64

The light from the overhead fixtures in the hall shone faintly into the tiny room, left as a storage area. It was bare except for one object that almost filled the space.

"Well, well," Joe said. "The missing case. And it's empty."

7 Fossil Fiasco

Frank and Joe exchanged surprised looks.

"That fossil didn't fly away," Joe said. "You think it could have been stolen?"

"I don't know," Frank murmured. He bent down to examine the side of the case. Joe squeezed into the small room to check the front.

"It looks like this top pops open in front." Joe wedged a finger beneath the edge of the sloping glass top. It swung up, turning on hidden hinges in the back. "There's no lock on it," Joe said.

Frank rose to scan the inside of the case. "There are a couple of clips here," he said. "The Archaeopteryx must have been anchored to this base. You can see where they've been unscrewed."

"Maybe Lubski took the fossil home with him," Joe suggested.

"Why would he do that?" Frank asked.

"I don't know. To study it?" Joe guessed.

"But that's what it's here at the museum for," Frank pointed out. "Besides, it was here earlier today, I'm sure. We know that Smith just sent Lubski home. Carl would have had to come back here just minutes ago to get it."

"So like I said, do you think it was stolen?" Joe said.

"And as *I* said, I don't know," Frank snapped. He ran a hand through his thick brown hair. "This place is full of scientists who might have some interest in the Archaeopteryx and reasons to move it." He turned to look around the Fossil Hall. "How about the rest of the hall? Has anything else been moved or is missing?"

"Let's check it out," Joe said. The two moved quickly through the room, checking this time for any other empty spaces. But everything looked the same, with all cases in place.

"So I guess it's just the one piece," Frank said. "Why?"

"Maybe this missing bird-thing has something to do with the accidents and mishaps around here." Joe frowned. "Maybe Parker took it and stashed it away someplace to drive Lubski crazy."

Frank was still deep in thought. Why move the whole display case? Then his eyes lit up. "Why don't we check the case for fingerprints?" he said. "That might give us a solid clue."

"Good idea," Joe said.

67

"I'll run to the van and get the fingerprint kit," Frank said. "Try to find Sally so we can show her the empty case."

The boys split up. Frank headed for the main entrance and the parking lot. Joe headed out the back, cutting through the dinosaur park to the administration wing.

Arriving at the offices, Joe hurried down the hall looking for Sally. Suddenly Clarence Smith's door flew open. The director barreled down the hall, almost walking into Joe.

"Oh—can I help you with something?" Smith asked, looking surprised.

"I was looking for Sally," Joe said.

"She's still in Bayport on some errands for the museum," Smith told him. "What's up?"

"I just wanted to tell her that one of the fossils seems to be missing from Lubski's exhibit," Joe said.

Smith's eyes flickered momentarily. "Missing? Which one?"

"The Archaeopteryx," Joe said.

"The Archaeopteryx?" Smith repeated in surprise. "Are you sure?"

"Yes, I—" Joe started.

"Oh, oh, wait a minute," Smith said, slapping a hand to his wide forehead. "I just remembered. Lubski said that it was being moved to the workshop. A cast is being made of it for another museum. It'll be back in the Fossil Hall before the opening." He shook his head with a weary smile. "With so many things to keep track of, the plan had slipped my mind."

"But I thought I saw the Archaeopteryx in the hall earlier today," Joe said, frowning. "We just noticed it missing a few moments ago."

Smith shrugged. "They probably moved it this afternoon. I'm afraid I don't remember all the details." He smiled at Joe. "Copies are often made of important fossils. Sometimes museums exchange them, sometimes they're sold. I'm sorry you were concerned. I do appreciate your vigilance, though."

Joe nodded and started back down the hall, then stopped. "I guess I just thought——"

Smith interrupted him with a chuckle. "You thought that Parker and Lubski were at it again, right?" he said.

"Well, yeah, actually——" Joe started.

"I don't blame you. Those two are like a pair of dogs, always testing each other's territory," Smith said. "But you learn to expect that when you're dealing with two good scientists."

"So you don't worry about their pranks and arguments and accidents?" Joe said, puzzled.

Smith held up a hand. "Of course I worry. It's my job to see they don't go too far. But there's bound to be a lot of tension less than two weeks before our opening."

Joe grinned. "So I notice."

"Just leave the worrying to me," Smith said.

69

"And again, I appreciate all you and your brother are doing for us."

Joe left the administrative wing and headed back to the Fossil Hall. Frank was carefully dusting the empty case for fingerprints.

"Hold the dust," Joe said, leaning in the doorway. "Dr. Smith says Lubski had the Archaeopteryx moved so it could be copied."

"Copied?" Frank said, putting down his brush.

Joe nodded. "For another museum."

Frank sighed. "I don't think we'd have gotten anything out of the fingerprints anyway. There must be two dozen different ones on this case."

"A lot of workmen have probably handled it," Joe said.

Frank began to pack away the equipment. "It would take us days to check them all out," he said.

"Nice try, though, Sherlock," Joe said.

Frank shot him a wry look. "Let's go see if Parker is back in the control shack. Maybe he's started testing the Dinobots again."

The brothers closed the closet door and went out to the dinosaur park. The sky was growing dark, but the Dinobots were still motionless, frozen in time. Winding their way through the machines, Frank and Joe checked the control shack. Parker wasn't there.

"Maybe he's in his lab," Joe said. But no one answered Joe's knock on the door, and the door was locked.

"I expect he went home," Frank said. "He looked

pretty frazzled after his Dinobot nearly flattened Lubski."

"I'm ready to call it a day, too," Joe said.

"Good call," Frank said. "Besides, I've got homework to do tonight."

"Homework?" Joe said.

"Yeah, you remember—those assignments teachers give at the end of class?" Frank teased.

Joe shook his head. "Doesn't ring a bell."

Frank sighed. "So I figured."

After a noon assembly at school the next day, Frank and Joe drove back to the museum. It was gray and windy outside, but the preserved world of the museum looked the same as it had the day before. The Hardys found Sally in her office.

"Any hot assignments today?" Joe asked.

Sally laughed. "I can't promise anything. How about heading over to the fossil lab?" She lowered her voice. "Lubski told me what happened with the Dinobot yesterday. I think he's embarrassed by his temper tantrum and wants to apologize."

"Sounds good," Joe said. "We're on our way."

Lubski was in his office in the lab, hunched over his computer. He looked as if he'd slept in his clothes, with his rumpled flannel shirt half tucked into wrinkled khaki pants. He glanced up as Frank and Joe appeared in the doorway.

"Please come in. I was hoping to talk to you." His deep voice seemed quieter and more measured than it had at the dinosaur park. "As if that wrangle

71

wasn't embarrassing enough, I never thanked you for your tackle, Frank. Thank heavens *one* of us had a cool head yesterday."

Frank grinned. "I'm glad I was there to do it," he said.

"I know it was an accident," Lubski said. He forced out a dry laugh. "Though I'm sure Parker would like to see me out of the way."

"Oh, I don't know," Frank said. "It seems as if Parker is just excited and worried about his Dinobot project."

"Actually, I feel sorry for Parker," Lubski said. "He's basically doing all these high-tech things to cover up his scientific inadequacies."

Frank and Joe looked at each other uncomfortably. *Here we go again*, Frank thought. "I think the public will enjoy both the fossil and the Dinobot exhibits," Joe put in.

Lubski shrugged. "I hope so. It's painful to put so much work into accurate scientific displays, then get pushed into the shadow by Parker's flashy toys."

"Well, uh . . ." Joe faltered. He wasn't sure what to say to the paleontologist. He had to admit to himself that he was a lot more interested in Parker's Dinobots.

"For me, pure science is all that counts," Lubski went on.

"Is there any help we can give you today?" Frank asked, hoping to change the subject. "Your fossils still need moving, don't they?"

"You're quite right," Lubski said. "If you'll wait

here for a moment, I'll check the progress in the Fossil Hall." He got up from his computer and went out of the office into the main hall.

Joe turned to Frank. "Whew," he said under his breath. "I don't think Parker and Lubski—"

"Aarrggh! No, no!"

An anguished cry from Carl Lubski cut off Joe's words.

8 A Crushing Case

Frank and Joe rushed into the Fossil Hall. Carl Lubski loomed over a small, freestanding fossil at the far end of the hall. His fists were clenched, and his frame was rigid with anger.

The boys ran over to the paleontologist. "What's wrong?" Joe said.

"This was one of my best specimens." Lubski's voice trembled with anger. "Now look at it."

Frank examined the collection of bones wired together to form a small primitive animal. The creature's head seemed much too large for its body, giving it a lopsided, almost comical, look.

"Someone switched skulls and bones with that fossil over there." Lubski stabbed a finger at a creature with a tiny head perched on a much bigger neck. "I can't take any more of these pranks."

74

"Can't you change them back?" Joe asked.

Lubski's eyes were blazing as he turned to Joe. "Of course I can," he snapped. "But that takes time. These bones are delicate. Plus, I'll have to check every fossil in the hall to make sure they haven't been tampered with."

Joe looked at Frank. Frank knew what he was thinking. The bone swap could be just another prank, perhaps by Parker. Certainly, it had provoked Lubski. But both Parker and Lubski were wrapped up in getting their exhibits ready. Neither seemed to have time to waste on jokes. So who else would be sneaking around the Fossil Hall?

Lubski stormed back to his office, Frank and Joe following. "These aren't toys, you know," the scientist bellowed. "Can you imagine the work that goes into retrieving and preserving just one bone?"

Obviously Lubski didn't expect an answer. Instead, Joe said, "Maybe the bones got shifted by accident by some of the workers."

"This was no accident," Lubski said firmly. "Everyone knows better than to touch the exhibits. No," he said nodding rapidly, "this was the work of someone out to get me. A certain Mr. Parker."

Joe stared at the fuming scientist. Was the guy paranoid, or was there really something malicious going on at the museum? "We don't know that for sure," Joe said carefully.

"Excuse me," a low voice at the doorway mumbled. Joe turned around to see Tom Smedly.

"What is it, Smedly?" Lubski asked.

The custodian's face reddened, and he shifted uncomfortably. "Uh—Dr. Smith wants me to move one of your skeletons to the storage building to make room for one of Mr. Parker's exhibits," he said quickly, the words coming out in a jumble.

"No!" Lubski exclaimed. "This is the last straw. I can't take it anymore. Parker can have this place—all of it!"

Smedly shrank back. "I—I'm sorry. But—"

"That's it!" Lubski interrupted. "I'm giving Smith my resignation—right now!" He brushed past Smedly and stormed through the Fossil Hall.

Frank and Joe began to follow him when the custodian said, "Uh, could you—"

The boys stopped. "Could we what?" Joe said.

"Could you help me with this move?" Smedly stammered. "I could use the extra hands."

"I'll stay," Joe told Frank. "You run after Lubski and see what happens."

Frank took off in Lubski's direction. By the time he entered the administrative wing, he could already hear raised voices down the hallway. Frank moved quietly toward the director's office. "You might as well turn this into a cartoon museum!" he heard Lubski shout.

"Calm down," Smith said, trying to be heard over Lubski's voice. "Please." The voices grew lower, and Frank could barely make out which man was speaking. He leaned toward the director's closed door, straining to hear.

"Quite a performance, wouldn't you say?" a

voice suddenly whispered in Frank's ear. Frank jumped in surprise and whirled around. Dan Parker stood behind him, a grin on his face.

"Mr. Parker!" Frank said. "I was just—"

"I know," Parker said. "I want to find out what's happening myself."

"Actually, I think it's about you," Frank said quietly. "Lubski thinks you sabotaged his fossil exhibit and he's boiling mad."

Parker's grin disappeared. "I wouldn't touch his old bones," he said. "Besides, I have far too much to do."

Frank cocked his head toward the door. The voices seemed to have stopped. Had they finished? "I don't think I ought to be here when they come out," Parker whispered.

Frank nodded and the two quietly headed down the hall. Back outside in the dinosaur park, Frank turned to Parker. "What started this feud between you and Lubski anyway?"

Parker shrugged. "Lubski is an ultraconservative paleontologist. He fights any new ideas. But he has a solid reputation, so Smith hired him to give scientific credence to the museum, hoping to get some government or university funding later on."

"And you represent the other side, I guess," Frank said. "Your exhibits are flashier, and Smith needs those to draw the general public."

"That's about right," Parker said. "I guess it was inevitable that Lubski and I should clash."

"But your rivalry goes way back, doesn't it?" Frank asked, remembering what Sally had said.

Parker readjusted his baseball cap. "Paleontology is a pretty small world," he said. "I used to do a lot of fossil collecting, too, so Lubski and I were competing for research money. Now that we're thrown together here at the museum, it's just made a bad situation worse."

With a wry smile, Parker began to head over to the control shack. Frank turned toward the Fossil Hall. "I've got to check on my brother and Smedly. We're helping him move some things."

Parker shook his head. "Poor Smedly. He's always so worried about things going wrong, and they usually do when he's around."

Frank grinned, remembering the light fixture. "I found that out the hard way."

"Well, when you're free, maybe you can give me a hand again with the Dinobots," Parker said.

"Sure," Frank said. He headed back into the Fossil Hall. There was no sign of either Joe or Smedly. Frank finally found them in the Hall of Prehistory.

"You're just in time," Joe said. "We're getting ready to move the bison sculpture."

"The bison case is being moved?" Frank asked.

"According to Smedly, Smith wants it moved," Joe said.

"How are we going to move this thing? It looks very heavy."

"I'll get a dolly," Smedly mumbled. "Be right back."

"So, did Lubski actually resign?" Joe said when the custodian had left.

"I don't know," Frank said. "He and Smith were going at it, but then I ran into Parker. We didn't want to get caught eavesdropping."

"Did you ask Parker about Lubski's fossils?" Joe said.

Frank nodded. "He looked like he couldn't believe Lubski was blaming him again." Frank heard a clanking sound and turned to see Smedly rolling a large dolly into the hall.

"That might work," Joe said. He moved to one side as Smedly placed the dolly in front of the case. "Frank, you grab that side of the case, and I'll take this one," Joe said. "We'll see if we can shift it onto the dolly. Smedly, try to hold the dolly still."

The custodian nodded, and Frank and Joe wrapped their arms around the sides of the case. Carefully, they lifted the edge of the case and, with a final heave, were able to slide it all the way to the dolly's frame.

"Piece of cake," Joe said, breathing heavily.

"Where does it go now?" Frank asked Smedly.

"On the other side of the hall somewhere. I have it written down," Smedly said, going through his pockets. He sighed. "I must have left my note in the other building."

"But you're sure it goes on the other side?" Joe said.

"Pretty sure. I'll go get the paper," Smedly said, running out again.

"At least we can start moving this thing," Frank said. He began to push the dolly forward.

The dolly stopped in a screech of metal as one of its left wheels went spinning out onto the floor. Still holding the dolly, Frank made a wild grab at the case to keep it from sliding off.

But he was too late. The case had been jarred from its spot. Now it slid into Joe, knocking him backward. Frank lunged for the other side of the case as it tipped precariously toward Joe, about to crush him.

9 Night Prowlers

"Yow!" Joe yelled. "Watch that thing!"

Frank's muscles strained as he struggled against the weight of the case. But he could feel it slipping from his fingers.

Suddenly, other hands appeared on the case. Frank looked up to see Parker pulling beside him. They hung on, fighting the heavy, bulky object, freezing it in midfall. But even with both of them, the case was too heavy to be pushed back onto the dolly.

From the corner of his eye, Frank saw Smedley running across the Hall of Prehistory. At the same time, Joe rolled away from the teetering case. With Smedley pushing and Frank and Parker pulling, they eased the case upright.

Frank kicked the broken dolly out of the way.

Finally, the case creaked back to a standing steady rest.

"Nice save," Joe said. "A few more inches and you'd have been preserving *me* for the museum."

"I'm glad you showed up when you did," Frank told Parker, flexing his fingers to get some feeling back into them.

"Me, too," Parker said. "I only came in here to see if you boys were available."

"I wasn't here when the case fell off the dolly," Smedly quickly said to Parker. "I had nothing to do with it. I didn't know the dolly was broke."

Parker gave Smedly a puzzled look. "It's okay. No one is accusing you of anything."

Frank retrieved the wheel that had detached itself. "I wonder why this came off?" he said. "Maybe the case was too heavy for the dolly."

"Unh-uh!" Joe knelt on the floor, examining the dolly axle. "Looks like the nut that held the wheel in place fell off or was never there."

At the same time, Smedly and Parker took small wrenches from their back pockets. Parker grinned. "I guess working here teaches you to be prepared."

"I'll get it," Smedly said hurriedly. "I always carry some extra nuts and bolts."

The custodian quickly secured the wheel with twists of his wrench.

Taking no chances this time, Frank dropped to one knee and checked the tightness of the nut that now held the wheel in place.

"Let's see how the sculpture made out," Parker

said. He popped open the glass door atop the display case, and the four of them looked at the bison sculpture. Parker reached in and felt the clips holding it in the case.

"Jostled a little loose at the base," he said. "But otherwise it looks all right."

"What's that?" Frank said. "It looks like a piece broke off." He pointed to a corner of the case.

Parker grabbed the small, dark-colored piece of clay. He turned it over in his hand, scowling at it.

"Do you think it can be reattached?" Frank asked.

"Huh? Reattached? Oh, no problem," Parker answered absently. Smedly's smile disappeared as the scientist examined the clay chip. Frank watched the familiar nervous look return as the custodian began wiping a bandanna over his brow.

"Since we're all here, let's move the case where Dr. Smith wants it," Frank suggested.

"Good idea," Parker said. Smedly pulled a piece of paper from his pocket. "Right over there," he said, pointing to the wall farthest from them. Frank pushed the dolly while the other three held onto the sides. In moments, they had rolled the case to its new location.

"Uh, thanks for your help," Smedly said, his eyes on the floor. "I've got to bring this back." He quickly wheeled the dolly out of the room.

Parker turned to the Hardys. "Joe, you look a bit shaky. Why don't you guys take a break and grab a bite to eat? I'll meet you back at the control shack."

"Sounds good. Maybe I got knocked harder than I thought," Joe admitted. "See you in an hour or so."

At the diner in Sackville Corners, the Hardys sat in a booth and attacked roast beef sandwiches. "Forget about prehistory," Joe said. "They should call that place the Museum of Accidents. Every time we turn around there's something falling apart or breaking or mysteriously moving."

"Coincidence?" Frank said, pausing before a bite.

Joe shook his head. "What else can it be? Maybe Lubski and Parker hate each others' guts, but each of them denies hurting the other's exhibit. Besides, sabotage just doesn't make sense for either of them. It just delays the museum opening and hurts both of them."

"Unless"—Frank looked at Joe carefully—"someone wants to keep the museum from opening."

"Why would anyone want to do that?" Joe asked.

"That's what we have to find out," Frank replied with a shrug.

They ate in silence for a while. Then Joe said, "What do you think of Smedly? Like Parker said, there always seems to be some mishap when he's around."

He always seems nervous, which is enough to make somebody clumsy." Frank stopped. "But *why*

84

is he nervous? Maybe we can find out something from his personnel file."

"Through Sally?" Joe said.

Frank shook his head. "Let's not get her into trouble. I'll give it a shot later tonight."

Joe frowned. "There's a watchman who makes the rounds at night. Why don't we just keep an eye on Smedly after he gets off work?"

"Maybe we can do both," Frank said. "When Smedly leaves, we'll leave a minute or so after him. You can drop me off in the woods behind the museum to wait for dark, then follow Smedly."

Joe nodded. "I'm glad we have our pair of night-vision binoculars in the van. If you scan the museum grounds from the woods, you can keep track of the watchman's movements."

"Are you sure there's only one watchman?" Frank said.

"I think so," Joe said. "And I don't think there are any security cameras or alarms around. Since most of the exhibits aren't in place yet, I guess they're expensive for a museum on a tight budget."

"All the better," Frank said. "After you check out where Smedly goes, come back and park the van behind the woods. Give two short owl calls to tell me you're there. I'll answer with one 'whoo' to let you know where I am."

"Then we'll try the administrative wing's back door and get into the personnel office," Joe said.

"You got it," Frank said.

* * *

When they arrived back at the museum, Frank and Joe went to the control shack where Parker was waiting for them.

"You can help me tighten all the connections on the cables running from the Dinobots to the control panel," Parker said. "I've already started, but there are a lot of them."

The Hardys spent the rest of the afternoon helping the scientist check control cables. Joe worked from the center toward one side of the dinosaur park while Frank and Parker worked toward the other. Frank kept a close eye on his watch. He suspected Smedly was a real nine-to-fiver. He didn't want to lose him.

The three finished just before five, and Frank spoke quickly before Parker asked them to do anything further. "I guess that does it. We'll be back tomorrow, so let us know if you need us."

"I probably will," Parker said. "Thanks for your help. It would have taken me at least a day doing it by myself."

The boys hurried through the Hall of Prehistory and out the main entrance. Scanning the parking lot, Frank grabbed Joe's arm. "There he is." Joe followed Frank's gaze to a small, battered white pickup pulling out of a space near the end of the lot. Smedly was behind the wheel.

Frank and Joe jogged to their van and started after the custodian. Joe kept well behind the small truck as it turned out of the museum entrance toward Sackville Corners.

86

At the main highway, Joe pulled the van to the shoulder and Frank, carrying his night-vision binoculars, jumped out.

"Good luck," Joe said. "I'll meet you in the woods."

Joe lagged behind Smedly's pickup on the quiet streets of Sackville Corners. He came closer in traffic as the custodian pulled onto the road that went along the coast. Then Smedly turned off, heading through a neighborhood with manicured lawns and water views.

If this is where he lives, his custodian's job must pay pretty well, Joe thought.

At last, Smedly stopped at the gate of a large beach front house. Joe pulled up about a block away. The two-story house was gleaming white with a modern design. It was surrounded by a six-foot-high wall. Joe watched as the front gate opened and Smedly drove in.

Leaving his van, Joe walked cautiously toward the house. When he reached the gate, now closed, he noticed a bronze name plate on the wall: Raymond Casada.

Joe leapt, caught the top of the wall, and pulled himself up for a quick peek. As he did, he saw a curtain in one of the second-floor windows being pulled aside. The hulking form of a large man appeared at the window. Joe quickly dropped down again, hoping he hadn't been seen.

As he returned to the van, Joe weighed his

choices. He could circle around and approach the house from the beach side. Joe jogged through sand dunes that stretched from the highway to the beach. The dunes were too low for cover, but he hoped he was far enough away from the house not to be seen.

Reaching the water's edge, Joe looked back up the beach. He could see two tiny figures outside the house. Even at that distance, Joe recognized Smedly's slouch. The other figure was gesturing broadly toward the ocean. Joe wished he had a pair of high-powered binoculars. Still, he figured the other man must be Casada, whoever he was. Then, a slight woman with long red hair joined them. After a few minutes of talking, Joe watched as the three of them left the beach.

Joe hurried back, not wanting Smedly to pass the parked van and perhaps recognize it.

It's possible Smedly is doing a little moonlighting as a handyman, Joe thought as he drove back to Sackville Corners. *But then why were they hanging out on the beach?*

Stopping at the diner, Joe called his mother to tell her that he and Frank wouldn't be home for dinner. Then he waited in the diner until it was completely dark.

Joe drove back toward the museum and parked the van on a side road at the far end of the woods. He followed a dirt path through the woods, heading for the rear of the dinosaur park. Suddenly, a pair of headlights appeared behind him. Joe jumped into the bushes on the side and crouched down as the car went by.

The vehicle continued until Joe saw its lights go out about a hundred yards before the museum. Joe followed the trail. In a few moments, he came upon the car that had passed him. It was empty, parked among the trees.

When he reached the museum fence, Joe found himself behind the administrative wing. He climbed over, keeping to the edge of the woods until he'd circled around to the back of the dinosaur park. The Dinobots loomed large, casting long shadows in the dim light.

Joe crouched in the brush and gave two low *whoos*. He was answered a few seconds later by another *whoo*, only a few feet away. He crept over in the darkness, finally bumping into Frank.

"A car drove past me on the trail to the museum," Joe said in a whisper. "It's parked in the woods."

"Did you get a look at the driver?" Frank asked.

"No. But I think we should be extra careful," Joe said. "How about the night watchman?"

"He seems lazier than I expected. So far, he's only made the rounds once. The rest of the time he's stayed on the second floor of the administrative wing, watching television. You can even see the TV screen in the window."

"Let's hope all his favorite shows are on tonight," Joe said.

"We'll enter the administrative wing through the

back door. The personnel office is on the first floor, directly across the hall from Smith's office," Frank said.

"I'm right behind you," Joe said.

After Frank spent a few minutes with his lock-picking equipment, the door handle turned easily. He pushed it open a few inches, making sure there weren't any alarms to trigger. The offices were quiet, except for the faint sound of the TV set upstairs. The darkness was pierced only by the dim red light of the exit sign overhead.

Frank and Joe moved silently down the hall to the personnel office. Joe tried the door handle, and it swung open. Inside, Frank closed the door and played the beam of his tiny penlight around the room. It lit two desks stacked with papers and a row of file cabinets along one wall.

Frank and Joe headed for the cabinets. The top drawer of the middle one was labeled Personnel Files. Frank opened it and began riffling through the folders inside. They were arranged alphabetically and Frank stopped first at Lubski's.

Frank opened the folder and scanned through the paleontologist's résumé. "He's got degrees from several universities, even one from Oxford." Frank flipped through the pages of the résumé. "And he has dozens of published articles in scientific journals, years of field work, and many funded expeditions."

"Impressive," Joe murmured. "How about Parker?"

90

Frank returned Lubski's folder and opened Parker's. "He has a Master's degree and quite a few published articles, mostly in popular magazines. He was probably working for a Ph.D. when Lubski torpedoed him."

"I'll bet a lot of his articles are about the K/T extinction," Joe said.

Frank studied the sheet. "You're right."

"I knew it," Joe said. "What about Smedly?"

Frank shuffled through the folders. "I don't see his. Maybe it's filed out of order." He looked through again, stopping at every folder. "No, his file is definitely not here."

"Let's check the rest of the office and Smith's office, too," Joe said.

"We'd better hurry, though. My penlight is getting dim," Frank said.

The Hardys quickly shuffled through the papers on the two desks in the personnel office and scanned the drawers as well. As the penlight grew fainter and fainter, they checked Smith's desk across the hall.

"Nothing," Joe whispered as they left the building. "Smedly's getting more and more interesting."

He and Frank headed back toward the woods. The moon had risen, throwing shadows across the museum grounds. As they walked through the central park area, the Dinobots reflected the moonlight, sending off glimmers of light.

"Check it out," Joe whispered. Keeping to the shadows at the edge of the park, the Hardys stopped for a moment, gazing at the huge forms of the dinosaurs.

"It's like we've gone back in time," Frank murmured.

Suddenly Joe grabbed Frank's arm. "Look," he whispered fiercely. "Over there, at the Apatosaurus. Something moved."

Frank squinted in the dim light. "I don't see anything," he whispered back.

"Someone's there, I know it," Joe said. He took a step forward and tripped over something in the dark. From out of the darkness, a loud clanging sound rang out.

At the same moment, a dark figure raced out from beneath the legs of the Apatosaurus.

10 Out of Control!

"Quick! After him!" Joe shouted, stumbling to his feet.

The shadowy figure tore across the dinosaur park toward the fence by the woods. Frank could barely make out the dim form as it scaled the fence, then disappeared among the trees.

Joe raced after the intruder, the clanging noise still ringing in the background. Frank ran after him, trying to keep to the shadows in case the watchman responded quickly to the racket.

Joe leapt onto the fence, catching a brief flicker of movement on the path. But before he'd reached the top, they heard a car starting up. Its wheels spun on the sandy ground for a moment, then it roared away through the trees.

93

"That has to be the car that passed me earlier," Joe said.

"Did you get a decent glimpse of the person?" Frank asked.

"It looked exactly like—a shadow," Joe said glumly. "Sort of short, normal weight, nothing unusual." The clanging of the alarm had stopped, and now several lights had come on in the mansion.

"I thought you said there weren't any alarms," Frank whispered.

Joe shrugged. "It may have just been installed," he said. "Parker may have hooked something up himself to protect his Dinobots."

"Let's see if we can find out what this person was doing at the Apatosaurus," Frank suggested.

"Okay," Joe said. "But we'd better lay low for a bit."

From the edge of the woods, the boys watched as the guard made a quick search of the grounds. Keeping to the shadows, the Hardys managed to avoid the watchman's probing flashlight. Once he went back into the building, Frank and Joe saw each of the windows go dark as the watchman retraced his steps. They caught the blue flicker of the television go back on in the upstairs window of the administrative wing. The faint sound of canned TV laughter carried through the night air. The boys nodded silently at one another.

Guided by the moonlight, Frank and Joe hurried to the middle of the cluster of Dinobots. They prowled around the thick legs of the mechanical monsters, straining to see the ground.

"Look at this," Joe whispered tightly.

Frank turned to find Joe poking at a treelike Apatosaurus leg. The rubberized skin had been slit open, and someone had attempted to rip out the electrical wires underneath.

"Looks like our intruder was trying to sabotage the Dinobot," Joe said. "He probably got scared when I tripped the alarm."

"This is going way beyond pranks," Frank said. "Who wants to damage the Dinobots?"

"Lubski?" Joe said.

"He was mad enough at Parker today," Frank looked over his shoulder. "Let's see if we can find anything else." They crouched down, poking through the grass and bushes around the dinosaurs as well as checking the other Dinobots. But nothing turned up.

Frank found Joe in the darkness. "That watchman's got to be on another round now. Let's not press our luck." The two of them crept back through the museum grounds, scaled the fence, and found their way back to the van.

An hour later, the boys sat at their kitchen table over warmed-over chicken enchiladas. Fenton and Laura Hardy were in the living room, watching television, while Joe filled Frank in on Smedly's visit to Raymond Casada's house. The name wasn't familiar to Frank either.

95

Frank picked up one of the science magazines that Sally had brought over several nights before. "Research," she'd called it. He paged through, hoping to find some piece of information to shed light on the goings-on at the museum. He stopped at an article titled "The Art of Running Science Museums." His eyebrows rose as he read.

"Catch this," Frank said. "It's about the difficulties of museum curating. And it says that the professional reputation of the museum often determines the number of grants it can get."

Joe put his plate in the dishwasher and came over to read the article over Frank's shoulder. "I see bidding wars have sent the prices of prehistoric artifacts soaring."

Frank flipped through the other magazines. "Here's a piece on Clarence Smith," he said, scanning the article. "According to this, he's well respected but may have taken on too much with the prehistory museum. Sackville left a small fortune, but that's just not enough money. They're having severe financial difficulties."

"That's no surprise. Everyone at the museum complains about budget problems," Joe said. "Sally thinks there would be fewer accidents if they could hire more people."

"It can't help Smith to have his shaky finances made public like this. That could scare off potential funding sources," Frank said.

Joe nodded thoughtfully. "Maybe someone is *leaking* unfavorable information to the press."

"Hmmm," Frank said, reading on. "Did you know Smith was a paleontologist before switching to administration? This is his first time as a museum director."

"So I guess he has a lot riding on the success of the museum," Joe pointed out.

Frank nodded. *And where does that leave us?* he wondered.

Early the next afternoon, Frank pulled the van into the museum parking lot. A red compact car parked next to him, and Sally jumped out.

"Hey, you two," she said cheerily. She must not have heard about the damage to the Dinobot, Frank thought. She's in too good a mood. "Sorry I didn't get a chance to talk to you yesterday afternoon. I've been running errands like crazy. How is everything going?"

Frank shot Joe a warning look. Better not to say anything until they knew more.

Joe nodded at his brother, then gave Sally a big smile. "We're having more fun than you can imagine."

Sally looked at him suspiciously. "What does that mean? What have you found out since we talked the other night?" She glanced around, making sure their conversation was private.

"We've made a few interesting discoveries," Frank said. "But nothing definite. We'll fill you in when we know more."

"Okay," Sally said. "For now, why don't you see

how Dr. Smith is doing in the Hall of Prehistory? He's deciding what to do about the damaged bison sculpture. This is all so upsetting. He barely talked Lubski out of quitting yesterday, and now Lubski's favorite piece is broken." She shook her head. "Anyway, I'll be in my office if you have any questions about anything."

Sally headed for the administrative wing. As the Hardys walked over to the Hall of Prehistory, they decided to wait and see if there was any reaction to the damaged Dinobot. "If we act like we don't know anything about it," Frank said, "our saboteur may reveal himself."

Inside the Hall of Prehistory, they found Smith crouched down, peering inside a glass display case. Beside him knelt Michael Murray, the grad student the boys had met on their first day. As the Hardys got closer, they saw that Smith was studying the bison sculpture.

"I think it must be taken to the workshop," Smith said unhappily.

Murray hesitated. "But only a small piece is broken off. We could repair it right here and not risk damaging it further in a move."

Smith shook his head. "I want it repaired carefully and thoroughly. And since the sculpture will be on permanent display, it wouldn't hurt to use some special preservation techniques."

"All right," Murray gave in. "I'll see that it's moved to the workshop."

"Can we help?" Joe spoke up as the two boys approached. Smith and Murray glanced over.

"I'm sure Michael would appreciate that," Dr. Smith said.

Murray nodded. "There's no way I can do this by myself—not without its dropping again."

"Please!" Smith didn't laugh as he left the hall. "You're doing fine work," he told Frank and Joe. "Just be careful."

Murray turned to the Hardys with a shrug. "I'd have worked on the sculpture here for safety reasons, but I can hardly argue with the director."

"So where are we taking it?" Joe asked.

"There's a service building behind the control shack in the dinosaur park. It's a bit roomier than the lab, and some preservation jobs require strong chemicals."

He pointed to an unused dolly in the corner. "I guess we can use that, but we'll have to move the case gently, especially outside."

"First, let's double-check the dolly." Frank knelt and rattled each wheel. "They seem tight."

Carefully slipping the case on, they rolled the dolly to the door. Joe pushed while Frank and Murray held the sides to keep it steady.

Following the paths as much as possible, they slowly rolled the case to the service building. The workroom where they brought the case was a large, mostly empty space smelling faintly of wood shavings. A long workbench stretched along one wall with an assortment of tools hanging over it.

Frank, Joe, and Murray carefully slid the case off the dolly, leaving it in the center of the room.

"Perfect," Joe said. "No problem this time."

"Thanks for your help," Murray said. "I'll leave this here until I can get Lubski. Then he and I will work together on the restoration."

"Anything else we can do?" Joe asked.

Murray shrugged. "We're expecting a shipment of roof tiles this afternoon. Maybe you can help with that. Or you might check with Sally."

Murray left and Frank said, "I'll run over and see what Sally needs." A few minutes later, he returned, saying, "Well, we stay put. Sally wants us to help with that tile shipment."

The two of them went around to the front of the service building and waited outside until a truck pulled up. Two large, tanned men got out and lowered a ramp on the back of the truck.

"Hey, you guys here to help us unload?" one of them called over to Frank and Joe.

"That's us," Joe said. He and Frank went over to the back of the truck.

"Great," the man said. "My name's Tony. Jake will be on the roof with a rope and hoist. If you hand down the bundles of tiles from the truck, I'll put them on the carrier."

"Okay." Frank watched Jake use an extension ladder to climb onto the low-pitched roof of the service building. It was an older building, probably a garden storehouse back when the museum was the Sackville mansion. A large part of the roof was

100

bare. It looked as if older tiles had been ripped off to make room for the new ones.

Jake anchored the rope for the hoist, and they set to work. Over the next hour, they built up a rhythm. Frank would pick up a bundle of tiles inside the truck and hand it to Joe on the ramp. Joe would pass it down to Tony, who put it on the carrier at the end of the rope. Then Jake hauled it up. The truck was emptying quickly and the bundles were piling up on the roof.

"How about a break?" Tony yelled up to Jake.

"Sounds good." Jake climbed down, then rubbed his back. "Glad you guys are here. We left the warehouse with this load at seven this morning." He stretched, his back making popping sounds. "And that was *after* loading it at six."

Tony handed his partner a water bottle from the truck. Then he plopped down beside Frank and Joe, resting against the shaded wall of the shed. "So when's this place supposed to open?"

"Less than two weeks," Frank said. "There's still a lot of work to be done."

"They'll really have moving dinosaurs?" Jake gazed at the Dinobot heads soaring high above the roof of the service building. "I saw a news clip about them on television. Are they ready?"

"Just about," Joe said. "They may have to work out a few kinks." *And keep them from being sabotaged,* he thought. He wondered if Parker had seen the slashed Apatosaurus yet.

Jake's eyes widened, staring around the shed. "Hey, I think one of 'em is coming this way."

Joe smiled. "One of them can move a bit," he said. "But just back and forth a short distance."

Jake only looked more nervous. "A big guy with horns is definitely coming this way," he said. "And it doesn't look like he's stopping."

Tony laughed. "You're putting me on."

Chuckling, Joe pushed himself up and peered round the corner. His grin faded. "Jake's right. The Triceratops really is heading this way."

"It's *what?*" Frank leapt to his feet. The others had been right. The huge Dinobot was lumbering toward them. It wasn't moving very fast, but it made steady progress, like a slow-moving tank. And it was heading straight for the shed.

"Where's Parker?" Frank said.

Joe stared at the Triceratops coming ever closer. "I hope he's inside that thing and knows what he's doing."

But it didn't seem so. The four horrified onlookers scattered as the Dinobot reached the side of the service building. It didn't stop. One horn on the Triceratops hit the wall, and the machine veered to the right a bit. But as Frank watched in disbelief, the machine stomped through the building, splintering its wooden frame. The roof smashed in, and bundles of roof tiles came cascading down. Chunks of wood and tools went flying. The Dinobot plowed on, heading now for the fence surrounding the museum.

102

"We've got to stop that thing!" Joe yelled.

"Follow me!" Frank dashed after the Dinobot, which was actually dragging part of the building behind it. "The trapdoor to the cockpit is open underneath. I don't think anyone is inside."

Joe could see the small door beneath the dinosaur's belly flapping a couple of feet above the ground as the Triceratops moved. And it kept moving, tearing through the chain-link fence as if the fence were paper. Then it was in the woods, knocking down a small tree in its path.

"Mr. Parker!" Joe yelled. But his voice was lost in the low rumbling of the machine.

Suddenly, the Dinobot ran into a large oak tree and came to a halt. The boys could hear the gears grinding inside the Dinobot as it struggled to push the tree over. The tree shook and shuddered, looking as if it were about to give way.

"I'm gonna get inside and turn it off," Joe yelled, pulling ahead.

"It's too dangerous," Frank yelled back.

"We don't have a choice," Joe said. "Quick! Boost me through the trapdoor."

The Hardys reached the temporarily stalled Dinobot. The engine roar grew louder as they positioned themselves beneath the dinosaur's underbelly, just below the swinging trapdoor. Frank gave Joe a boost up into the cockpit, where Joe managed to squeeze into the small bucket seat in front of the controls.

Frank leapt away from the huge legs of the

103

mechanical beast just as the oak gave way. It toppled over with a terrible ripping sound and the Dinobot lurched forward again.

Inside the loud, jerking Dinobot, Joe scanned the control panel in front of him for the off switch. There were several buttons, none of them marked. In desperation, Joe pushed all of them. The Dinobot didn't stop but began to thrash its tail back and forth and move its head from side to side, tearing branches off nearby trees.

Joe could feel a trickle of sweat move down his forehead. *What now?*

He looked at the small television monitor on the control panel in front of him. His heart dropped like a rock. On the fuzzy black and white monitor he could see the patch of woods directly in the Dinobot's path.

But in front of them, only a few feet away, was a large pond. It looked deep enough to short-circuit the machine's electric systems—not to mention fry anyone trapped on board.

11 Over the Edge

Joe knew he had only seconds before the Dinobot plunged into the pond, taking him with it. If he couldn't stop it, he'd somehow have to make the triceratops turn.

Joe grabbed the joystick and pushed it hard to the right. With a jerk, the Dinobot lumbered into a slow turn. But a quick look at the screen told Joe it was turning too slowly to miss the pond.

Still holding the joystick, Joe felt his fingers slide over a knob on its underside. Instinctively, he turned it. As he did, the Dinobot came to an abrupt, creaking halt, its right forefoot sinking into the ooze at the edge of the pond. The rumbling noise died suddenly.

Joe let out a sigh of relief. He should have known

that the stop mechanism would be someplace in easy reach.

Soaked with sweat, Joe wriggled from the bucket seat and out the trapdoor. He landed on all fours beneath the still Dinobot. Frank was already there to help him up.

"Nice stop," Frank said. "I thought you were going to get your feet wet."

"Me, too," Joe said. "And I don't think this thing swims." The two of them stared back along the path of destruction left by the Dinobot. Trees were smashed, the museum fence was mangled, and the service building looked as if a hurricane had hit it. Only one wall was left standing.

"It wiped out the whole building," Joe said in awe.

"And the bison sculpture inside it." Frank stared at the flattened building thoughtfully as he and Joe headed out of the woods.

They reached the shed to find Smith and Lubski standing in front, near the roofers' truck. Lubski and Smith wore the same horrified expression. Their mouths were open and their eyes were wide as they surveyed the damage. Jake was inside the wreckage, trying to salvage as many tiles as he could find. Tony was carrying them back to the truck.

"Guess you were right," Tony said, passing the boys with an armful of tiles. "They *do* need to work some kinks out of those dinosaurs."

Sally dashed up behind Frank and Joe, out of breath. "Smedly's hurt! I think he was hit by the

Dinobot. He's at the edge of the dinosaur park,"
she said in a rush. She turned to run back to the
park with the Hardys following. Just before they
reached the cluster of dinosaurs, they found
Smedly on the ground, moaning. He had a nasty
gash on the side of his head.

"I'm afraid he's pretty out of it," Sally said. "See
if you can bring him around. I'll run over to
administration and get the first aid kit."

Frank and Joe knelt over the custodian. "Smedly.
Smedly, can you hear me?" Frank said.

Smedly's pale, grizzled face twisted back and
forth. "Wha—what happened?" he asked, not
opening his eyes.

"You were hurt," Frank said. "Anything feel
broken?"

"I don't think so," Smedly muttered.

In a minute, Sally was back with the first aid kit.
Frank and Joe helped her bandage the cut on
Smedly's head.

"Ooh," Smedly groaned. "My head." His eyelids
flickered, and he finally looked at them.

"It's all right," Sally said. "We'll get you to a
hospital."

"I think the nearest one is Bayport General," Joe
said.

"Let's call an ambulance then," Sally said.

"We can take him," a voice said behind her.
Frank glanced up to see Jake and Tony standing
over Sally, looking down at Smedly. "We gotta go
through Bayport anyway," Tony said. "There's

plenty of room in the truck—most of the tiles are ruined. Jake'll look after him."

"Sure thing," Jake said. "I've had plenty of concussions myself. I know how the guy feels."

Within minutes, Tony had backed the truck to the edge of the dinosaur park. After making sure nothing was broken, Frank and Joe helped a shaky Smedly to his feet, placing him carefully into the back of the truck. Sally ran up with a blanket and had Smedly lie down on it.

"Take him straight to the emergency room," Sally said to Tony. "And thanks for your help."

Dr. Smith silently watched Smedly get lifted into the truck. Now he turned to Tony and Jake. "You can tell the emergency room physician I'll be there later to check on Smedly," he said. He shook his head. "I hope our insurance covers this."

The truck took off down the museum drive. Sally and Dr. Smith headed back for the service building, picking through pieces of wood and tools that were scattered about.

The Hardys hung back. "You know, someone had to start up that Triceratops," Joe murmured.

Frank nodded. "And who was the only one around the dinosaur park when it happened?" he asked as if he already knew the answer.

"Smedly," Joe said. "Getting stomped on by a huge piece of machinery wouldn't leave a gash on his head. It looks like he got clipped by something sharp, say, a swinging trapdoor."

Frank stared at the crushed service building.

108

"So, Smedly starts the Dinobot and aims it for the service building," he said. "Then he has to bail out before the collision."

Joe nodded. "Yeah, a jump through a small opening on a moving machine. Smedly tries but hits his head on the trapdoor on the way out."

"You explained everything but *why*," Frank said. "Why would Smedly want to destroy the service building?"

Joe shrugged. "Let's see if we can find anything." They joined Smith, Sally, and Lubski, who were picking through the wreckage.

"Now do you see why I'm worried about these mechanical toys?" Lubski was telling Dr. Smith. "Even if you have an area roped off, one of them can go haywire and create all kinds of havoc."

Smith sighed. "I guess you're right," he said. "Parker will have to stick to the dinosaurs that just move their heads and tails."

Lubski looked surprised. It was probably the first time he had made a suggestion that hadn't been followed by an argument. "I'm glad you agree," he said.

"Have you found anything in the debris?" Smith asked him.

"Just a few small tools," Lubski replied. "I'll take them over to my lab where they'll be safe." He hurried across the grass toward his laboratory.

Smith picked up a board as Lubski walk away, revealing the smashed bison sculpture. Deftly, he picked up broken pieces of clay, slipping them into

109

a small paper bag. Frank was about to ask the director if he needed help, but Smith seemed totally absorbed in his task. After collecting most of the pieces, he put the small bag into a larger collection bag.

Lubski returned to the disaster site. "Have you seen Parker around?" Smith asked. "I'd like some explanation about this runaway dinosaur."

"No, I didn't see him," Lubski said.

Sally looked up from where she had been sifting through some tools. "I believe he's in Bayport getting supplies," she said.

Lubski let out a short, sarcastic laugh. "Maybe he's picking up some brakes for his pathetic machines."

"Enough, Carl. You've made your point, or rather, the Triceratops has made it for you." Smith sighed. "It's too bad. The mobile dinosaur would have been such an attraction for the public." Smith rose, gripping the collection bag. "Sally, if you need me, I'll be in my office."

"I've got to get back to work, too," Lubski said. He headed toward the Fossil Hall.

Sally turned to the Hardys. "I think we've salvaged about everything we could," she said. "This building will have to be completely rebuilt. Just what we need on our tight budget. At least Dr. Smith seems to be taking it pretty well."

Frank looked around the area. Some workers and volunteers had joined them, piling up the debris so that it could be carted off. "Sally, can we talk to you privately?" he asked. "We have a few things to run by you."

Sally checked her watch. "The day's almost done, and I could use a cup of tea," she said. "Suppose we meet at the diner in half an hour?"

"We'll be there," Frank said.

At the diner the boys discussed the case. "Parker was in town most of the day," Frank said, "which explains why there wasn't a blowup over the slashed Apatosaurus leg." Just then, Sally appeared at their table. Joe slid over in his seat in a booth near the rear of the diner to make room for Sally. "We ordered your tea," he said.

She stared at the mound of french fries on the plate in front of Joe. "What's that?" she said.

Frank smiled. "That's Joe's idea of a light snack," he said.

Joe shrugged. "Help yourself," he said.

Sally shook her head with a smile. "No, thanks. What have you guys found out?"

"First of all, does the name Casada mean anything to you?" Frank asked.

Sally took her tea from the waitress. "Casada? Oh, yes," she said. "He's a wealthy antiques dealer. I hear he's also suspected of dealing in forgeries and stolen artifacts."

Joe shot Frank a quick look. "I followed Smedly to Casada's beachfront estate," he said.

Sally stared. "You're kidding! What would Smedly be doing at Casada's?"

"That's what we'd like to know," Frank said. "Smedly's turning into quite the man of mystery. Do you know he has no employment records?"

"He could have taken them," Sally mused. "After all, he cleans up the personnel office."

"Definitely possible," Joe said. "Can you think of any reason *why* he'd do that?"

"No," Sally admitted. "Unless he's trying to hide something on his records—something he doesn't want us to know about."

"Maybe they show some connection with Casada," Joe suggested.

"But if he has a bad record, why would Smith hire him in the first place?" Frank asked.

Sally blinked in confusion. "Tom Smedly—involved in something illegal with Casada? I can't imagine poor Tom doing anything like that."

"Well, we'd better start imagining *something*," Frank said. "How about Smith? Do you know if he's had any dealings with this Casada?"

"I don't think Smith would want *any* involvement with Casada. But . . . I really don't know." She sighed. "I wish I could help you."

"You have," Frank said. "You told us who Casada is, and you see how many possibilities that opens."

"Too many." Sally looked uncomfortable. "But if you hear anything else, let me know. I'll try to keep my eyes open around the museum. Despite the lax security."

* * *

It was almost dark when the boys headed home. "So," Frank said. "Smedly visits a shady type who deals in stolen artifacts. He also works at a museum where he has access to valuable exhibits. What kind of connection would *you* draw?"

"Let's start with the obvious one. Smedly has been swiping stuff from the museum and selling it to Casada," Joe replied. "But I don't remember hearing about any thefts from the museum."

"Me neither," Frank said. "The missing Archae-opteryx was a false alarm."

"We suspect something is going on between Smedly and Casada," Joe said. "We also suspect that Smedly's the one who started up that Triceratops. How do these two things fit together?"

"I wish I knew," Frank said, lost in thought.

By now they were a couple of miles out of Sackville Corners. Joe squinted as headlights reflected off the rearview mirror. "This guy is sure in a hurry to pass," he said.

"Well, he's got the whole road," Frank said. "There's not much traffic tonight."

"I don't think he knows that," Joe said.

The vehicle quickly caught up with the van, then pulled alongside. Joe looked over and saw that it was a pickup truck, whose driver wore a ski mask. As the boys stared in disbelief, the truck swerved into the side of their van.

"Hey!" Joe exclaimed, veering to avoid the pickup. "He's trying to drive us off the road!"

113

"Hit the brake!" Frank yelled.

Before Joe could react, the pickup truck swerved again. It brushed against the van, pushing it to the side of the road.

The van hurtled across the shoulder toward the edge of a high embankment!

12 An After-Hours Intruder

"Hold on!" Joe shouted, fighting the wheel. He pumped the brakes as the van swerved sideways and skidded on the dirt at the side of the road. The pickup sped past them, disappearing in the dark.

The next thing the boys heard was a thud and the sound of impacted metal. The van jarred to a stop, flinging Frank and Joe forward against their seat belts.

Joe still gripped the steering wheel. "What happened?" he said.

"I think we sideswiped a pole," Frank said.

Joe groaned. "Not another dent in that side of the van."

The Hardys unhooked their seat belts and climbed out of the van. It was at the edge of the shoulder, leaning against a metal light pole. The van's right wheels were in a little ditch a few inches from the drop-off.

"I guess we really can't complain," Frank said quietly. The light pole they'd hit was the only thing between them and a thirty-foot drop down a steep embankment.

"Whoever was driving that truck picked the right spot," Frank said. "Looks like they meant to get rid of us for good."

Joe glared down the dark highway. "Check it out," he said.

Frank's anger rose as he made out the pickup, which had pulled onto the shoulder a couple of hundred feet ahead. He could see the red brake lights shining in the dark but couldn't make out the license number.

"Guess he wants to make sure he won this demolition derby," Joe said. In a moment, the lights of the truck moved back onto the highway, and it sped away into the distance.

Joe walked around the side of the van, checking for damage from the pole. There was an indentation a few inches deep, and the paint had been scraped away. "Not too bad," he said. "We can knock that out. The van was due for a paint job anyway."

Joe headed around to the driver's side. "I'll put her in low gear," he said. "Give me a push from the back."

Joe started the engine and slowly released the brake. The wheels spun for a moment as Frank added a strong push. The van slid out of the ditch. Frank ran up and jumped in the passenger side, and they headed down the road.

Joe moved the steering wheel back and forth in small motions. "The van seems to be handling all right," he said. "No major damage. I could try to catch up with that driver," he suggested.

"That pickup is long gone." Frank shook his head, then glanced at Joe. "But I suddenly recall a proud pickup owner we've seen recently."

"Smedly." Joe chimed in, nodding. "There's more than that. This guy wore a ski mask with a bandanna tied around his neck."

"And Smedly's always got a bandanna," Frank finished.

"But we saw Tony and Jake take Smedly to the emergency room just a few hours ago," Joe said.

"His injury wasn't very serious," Frank noted. "They could have patched him up and released him."

"Why would Smedly want to kill us?" Joe asked.

"Maybe he recognized you at Casada's house," Frank suggested.

Joe shook his head. "I don't think so. Besides, it wasn't as though I caught him doing anything. He was just talking to Casada."

"Maybe we're getting close to something Smedly doesn't want us to know about," Frank said.

"What?" Joe said.

Frank frowned in thought. "I wish I knew."

* * *

117

As soon as they arrived home, Frank grabbed the phone book in the hallway to get the number of the hospital. Quickly, he dialed the phone.

"Hello, Bayport General," a woman's pleasant voice answered.

"Could you tell me if you have a patient there named Thomas Smedly?" Frank asked.

"Hold on," the woman said.

After a couple of minutes, she came back on the line. "I'm sorry, we have no patient here by that name."

"One more question," Frank said. "Could you see if he was treated in your emergency room this afternoon?"

"I'll try," she said.

After another short wait, she said, "Yes, a man by that name was treated in the emergency room. He was held for observation for about an hour, then released."

"Thanks," Frank said. He turned to Joe, who stood behind him. "Smedly was released hours ago."

Their parents had gone out for the evening, so Frank and Joe ate the homemade soup and bread their mother had left for them in the kitchen.

Frank had been deep in thought since he sat down. Finally, he said, "Did Dr. Smith seem odd to you this afternoon?"

"What do you mean?" Joe said.

"I'm not sure," Frank admitted. "He was so calm. Even Sally noticed. I mean, the workshop had just

118

been wasted, his prize bison sculpture ruined, and he's walking around, quietly putting the pieces in a bag."

"I thought he'd really flip over that bison," Joe admitted. "Maybe he was in shock."

Frank nodded, frowning. "And why did he pick up all the pieces himself? He left everything else to Sally, Lubski, and us."

"I guess he needed them to show to the insurance company," Joe said.

"Maybe," Frank admitted. "But it was as if he expected the bison to be broken. He didn't say anything; he just started collecting pieces."

"What a case!" Joe burst out. "Lubski wants to stop Parker. Parker wants to hurt Lubski. Smedly wants to foul up everyone. Now you're saying *Smith* wants his own museum to fail, smashing his prize exhibit. That doesn't make sense. The thing is priceless."

"If it's the *real thing*, it's priceless," Frank countered. "If not, it's like breaking a water glass. You sweep up the pieces and go on."

Joe's eyes lit up. "You think the bison sculpture might have been a forgery?"

Frank shrugged, a little smile on his lips. "That would explain Smith's calm reaction. Maybe that's how Casada fits into this weird puzzle."

"And with the sculpture destroyed," Joe added excitedly, "no one can *prove* it was fake."

Frank nodded, his mind whirling. "So we've got to find some way to do that."

"How about finding a piece of the bison sculpture in the wreckage of the building?" Joe said. "Then we could have it analyzed."

"I think Smith probably got all the big chunks. Any tiny pieces he didn't find are probably just dust by now," Frank said.

"Do you think he still has them, like in his office?" Joe gave his brother an angelic smile.

Frank caught the gleam in Joe's eye. "Guess there's only one way to find out," he said to his brother. He sighed. "I'm beginning to feel like Sally. The museum is becoming our home away from home."

Frank parked the van just off the road near the museum. He and Joe crept through the dark woods to the back of the administrative wing.

"It seems like I've been through this before," Joe whispered.

"Me, too," Frank said. "But it shouldn't take us long. We know exactly what we're looking for. If we don't find it right away, we leave."

Once again, Frank picked the lock on the door. They slipped inside and walked quietly down the hall to Smith's office. Frank listened for the sound of the night watchman's television set upstairs. But there was only silence. His heart began to beat faster. The guard could be on his rounds, perhaps starting right here.

The door to Smith's office was partially open. Frank and Joe stopped in the hallway, listening

120

carefully. Soon Frank could make out some faint clinking sounds coming from inside the office. Then a very dim light blinked off and on.

Frank's eyebrows shot up in surprise. It looked like the sort of dim beam thrown by a penlight. The watchman wouldn't need that. He could turn on the room lights if he wanted to see.

Frank's hands turned to fists. Someone was in Smith's office, someone who was trying to keep his or her presence a secret.

13 Caught in the Act

Frank clenched the large flashlight he'd brought for searching. Now it had a better use.

He stepped into the office, aiming his flash. Its beam illuminated a figure crouched in front of Smith's open safe.

A man whirled around, shielding his eyes against the flashlight beam. It was Dan Parker.

"Parker!" Joe exclaimed from behind Frank.

"Joe? Frank? Is that you guys?" Parker said, squinting into the strong beam.

Frank lowered the flashlight. "That's right," he said. "You tell us why you're here and we'll tell you our story."

"I think we're probably here for the same reason," Parker said. He held up a small paper bag, the one Smith had used earlier in the day to collect the bison sculpture fragments. "We all want to get a piece of this clay."

"That's right," Joe blurted out. "We want it analyzed to see if the sculpture was a fake."

"I'm pretty sure it was," Parker said. "I think Lubski wanted to destroy that bison to keep anyone from knowing it was a fake—and he used my Dinobot to do it."

"What makes you think the sculpture wasn't real?" Frank asked.

"Remember how a chip came off when the case fell from the dolly in the Hall of Prehistory?" Parker said. "I examined it and realized something. The interior of the sculpture didn't look as old as the surface seemed. In fact, it looked way too new. If the bison were genuine, the effects of aging would show all the way through the piece."

"But what would Lubski have to gain by destroying the sculpture?" Joe asked.

"It's simple. Elsa Mansfield has been away, so Lubski was doing the purchasing for the museum. I think he found out that the sculpture he bought was a fake. Rather than look foolish, he tried to hide his mistake by destroying the sculpture." Parker scowled. "And who better to blame the destruction on than me and my Dinobots?

"But his little plan backfired," the furious Parker went on. "I'm going to discredit him the way he ruined me years ago. I'll get one of these pieces tested. A friend of mine can do it."

"Do you think Lubski told Smith what he was doing?" Frank asked.

"No," Parker said. "I think Smith picked up the pieces to show to the insurance company."

"How did you know that Smith picked up the pieces?" Joe asked.

"From Sally. She gave me the whole disastrous story when I got back here just before closing."

"Did she mention that Smith waited until Lubski wasn't there to gather up the fragments?" Joe asked.

"No." Parker looked surprised. "I'd expect Lubski to have stayed to watch over everything."

"Maybe Lubski isn't the one behind this," Frank said. "If your theory is correct, he went through a lot of work to avoid a little embarrassment. I think there must be something more."

"But it was also a way to get at me," Parker insisted stubbornly. "I'm sure Lubski is at the bottom of this. Do you have a better theory?"

"We think that a crooked antiques dealer named Casada is involved somehow and that Smedly may be connected as well," Frank said.

"If Smedly's in on it, he must be working for Lubski," Parker said. "I don't think he's bright enough to be the mastermind."

"Right now, we've got almost as many puzzle pieces as there are bison fragments," Frank said. "Let's get one of these clay chips tested and make sure the sculpture *was* a fake. Then we can start fitting the rest of our theories together."

Parker nodded. "My friend Helen Rogers is a technician in a dental lab in Bayport," Parker said. "She can tell us."

"A dental technician?" Joe said dubiously.

"That's just her day job. Helen has a Master's degree in micropaleontology," Parker explained. "The lab is downtown on Market Street by the courthouse. Why don't you meet me there in the morning?"

"Will she be there on a Saturday?" Frank asked.

Parker smiled. "Her schedule's like mine—Saturday is just another workday. We can meet at nine-thirty. I'll take one of the bison pieces for tests and put the rest back in the safe."

"By the way," Joe said, "how did you manage to get Smith's safe open?"

"Just luck," Parker admitted. "Smith had closed the safe, but he forgot to twirl the dial."

"Lucky for all of us," Frank said.

Parker put the bag with the rest of the fragments back in the safe and closed the door, then turned the dial. Frank turned off his beam and they all left Smith's office.

As they reached the exit from the office wing, the door suddenly opened from the other side. The uniformed night watchman leapt back with a start when he saw the three of them.

"Mr. Parker," he said in surprise. "I thought you left a long time ago. And I didn't know you had people with you."

"My assistants and I were finishing up a few

things on overtime, Murphy," Parker said smoothly. "You know what a tight schedule we have. We left some papers for Smith on his desk. He needs them first thing in the morning."

"You didn't need to come all the way over here," Murphy said. "I could have brought the papers over for you."

"Thanks anyway, Murphy," Parker said. "I didn't want to bother you."

"I'll have to open the front gate," Murphy said. "I locked it when I thought you had left."

"Thanks," Parker said.

The night watchman let them out and Frank and Joe walked with Parker up the road. "I'll call Helen Rogers tonight and tell her we'll meet her in the morning," Parker said.

"And we'll let Sally know that we'll be a bit late in the morning," Frank said. He and Joe said good night to the scientist and headed home.

The next morning, Frank and Joe met Parker in front of the modern-looking one-story building where the dental lab was located. Inside, the lab seemed to be a dark maze of offices, brightened only by the panel of windows facing Market Street.

"We're here to see Helen Rogers," Parker told the receptionist when they went in.

"Helen is expecting you. Go straight down the hallway. Her lab is at the end."

A short blond woman met them at the last door

126

along the hall. Parker smiled. "Helen Rogers, meet Frank and Joe Hardy."

"Dan, it's good to see you again," she said.

"I hope I'm not upsetting your routine with this," Parker said.

"Not at all," Helen said. "It's nice to have some work in my chosen field for a change. You brought along the sample?"

"Here it is," Parker said, taking a small box from his pocket. He opened it. "Is this enough?"

Helen laughed. "I only need a speck," she said. "Remember, this is going under a microscope. Come into the lab."

They followed her into a clean white room filled with large pieces of equipment. Some of the apparatus had movable extensions sticking out like insect legs. Frank figured the instruments were used for making castings of fillings and artificial teeth.

"Over here." Helen led them to a binocular microscope. "I'll need some reference, too," she said, pulling a thick book off a well-filled shelf. "Each time period and each area of the earth has its own fossil fingerprints—remains of microscopic organisms that died and left their fossils in various geological strata. Depending on what I see, I can give you a date as well as determining where a specimen came from."

"Aren't there more accurate methods of dating?" Frank asked.

"There are," she said. "But I'd have to send the

sample out for a long time and it's very expensive. As Dan described this to me on the phone last night, the age of the clay is a moot point. I could easily find some clay that's ten thousand years old and sculpt it into anything."

"So what *can* you tell us?" Joe asked.

"Let's find out," Helen said, taking the sample from Parker. She scraped a small bit onto a glass slide and put it under the microscope. For long minutes, she examined the material, consulting her reference book from time to time.

"Any luck, Helen?" Parker asked.

"You say that this clay is supposed to be from southern France during the Ice Age?" she asked.

"That's right," Parker said.

Helen laughed. "Then you've got yourselves a fake."

Parker looked at Frank and Joe, raising his eyebrows.

"How can you tell?" Frank asked.

"There's pollen trapped in this clay. It comes from a particular plant, a plant that never grew in the south of France. I'd say the origin of this clay is closer to New England."

"Thanks for your time, Helen," Parker said. "This helps more than you know."

"Not at all," she said. "If you've got other projects at the museum where I can give a hand, just let me know."

Frank, Joe, and Parker left the dental building, stepping onto the busy, sunny sidewalk.

"How about some breakfast?" Parker said.

"Sounds good," Frank said. "There's a new coffee bar just down the street," he said.

They headed over to the coffee bar and picked up some juice and pastries. Sitting on a high stool, Joe put his elbows on the circular marble table. "Well, now we know for sure that the sculpture was a fake."

Parker nodded. "I've thought over what you told me—about this Casada somehow being involved. I bet Lubski got Smedly to help him steal the real sculpture. They had a copy made, and Lubski sold the real one to Casada, pocketing the money."

Frank quickly saw holes in this theory. "Lubski has his reputation as a paleontologist to consider. Would he risk years of hard work and his position at the museum for money?"

Parker silently stared out the coffee bar's windows. "You've got a point," he admitted. "Lubski's very serious about his science."

"All we know for sure is that Smedly did meet with Casada," Frank said. "Anything we may guess in connecting the fake sculpture to that meeting is just that—a guess."

"Do you think Sally knows something about the purchase of the bison sculpture?" Joe asked.

"She might," Parker said. "Let's call her at the museum and see if she'll meet us here."

Joe jumped up. "On my way." He returned frowning. "Smith answered my call. He said Sally wasn't there. I left a message that we're in town and did she have any errands for us here."

"I hope she gets the message soon," Frank said. "How much coffee will we have to drink to stall for time here?"

Twenty-five minutes later, Sally parked her car across the street from the coffee bar. Frank flagged her over to their table as she came in.

"Hi, Dan," she said as she pulled up a stool. "I didn't expect to see you here. Did you bump into these guys downtown and assign some work?"

"Uh, not exactly," Parker said.

"That's not really what this is about," Joe said. "I didn't want Smith or anyone else at the museum to know what we're up to."

Sally laughed. "So what *are* we up to?"

"We had a fragment from the bison sculpture tested this morning. It's a fake," Parker said.

"What?" Sally's mouth dropped open.

"We know Smedly met with this guy Casada, and we think it has something to do with the fake sculpture," Frank said. "Maybe Casada was buying the real one. But unless Smedly is secretly a paleontology expert, which I doubt, there must be a third person involved at the museum."

"Who?" Sally asked unhappily.

"Dan thinks it's Lubski," Frank said. "That's possible, but I don't think so."

Sally looked surprised. "Carl? Involved in faking a sculpture? I don't think so either."

"So that leaves Smith, some research assistants,

130

or some of the graduate students working around the museum," Parker said.

"It could even be someone from the outside," Joe said with a frown. "Your night watchman is very lax. Frank and I got in with no trouble."

"But I think anyone involved in the forgery of an artifact would probably know something about it," Parker pointed out.

"How do we find out who it is?" Sally asked.

"I think Casada holds the answer," Frank said. "He must know who Smedly is working with."

"He's hardly going to tell us," Parker said.

"I had something else in mind," Frank said. "Something with Sally's help."

"I don't like that look on your face," Sally said suspiciously. "What do you want me to do?"

"Just pretend that you're a potential buyer for some of Casada's wares," Frank replied. "Joe and I will go with you to his house. He doesn't know any of us. Maybe he'll say something or we'll see something that will give us a clue."

"I don't know," Sally said, hesitating. "Guys like Casada are very clever. They know how to protect themselves."

Frank shrugged. "I think it's worth a try."

"At the very least, you can size up Casada and see what kind of a person we're dealing with," Parker said.

"Somehow, I feel like I already know, and it gives me a queasy feeling." Sally took a deep breath. "But I'll go along with it. When will we try it?"

"How about now?" Frank said.

"Now?" Sally echoed.

"Just make an appointment," Frank said. "I got his number from the phone book." He handed her a slip of paper.

Sally sighed. "All right." She got up and went to the pay phone.

A few minutes later, she came back with a surprised look on her face. "Casada wants me to go out to his place this afternoon, about one o'clock. I didn't think it would be that easy."

Parker rose. "Well, let me know how it goes. And be careful. Who knows what Casada is up to?" Saying goodbye, he left the coffee bar, returning to the museum. Sally nervously picked at a muffin until it was time to go to Casada's.

"Let's take Sally's car," Frank suggested. "Our van may have been spotted at Casada's."

"Sure. I told Smith I'd be out running some errands anyway," Sally said.

They drove to Casada's beach house, following Joe's directions. As Sally pulled up at the gate. Frank noticed a small television camera scanning them. A speaker asked her to identify herself.

"Sally Jenkins to see Mr. Casada," she called out the window.

The electronically controlled gate swung open, and Sally drove to the front of the house.

As they stepped from the car, a large man opened the front door. Joe recognized him as the figure he'd seen in the upstairs window. He hoped the man wouldn't recognize him.

"Mr. Casada?" Sally asked.

"Mr. Casada awaits you." The man led them to a large, sunken living room decorated almost entirely in white. A slight, deeply tanned man rose from a snowy sofa. He had dark hair and eyes and looked to be about fifty.

"I'm Raymond Casada," the man said in a crisp, clipped voice. "Please come in."

"Thank you," Sally said as the three of them stepped carefully across the white carpeting.

"Would you like some tea?" Casada asked. "Otto, ten please." The large man bowed and left.

Frank looked around the airy room, which looked more like an art gallery. There were large tribal masks from the Sepik River in Borneo, Khmer carvings from Cambodia, and several Greek statues from the archaic period. Several large chairs and two oversized sofas circled a glass coffee table in the room's center.

Sally introduced Frank and Joe as her assistants and sank down on one of the sofas.

"You have a fascinating collection, I see," Sally said.

"Thank you," Casada said. "I pride myself on it. All the pieces are for sale, however."

"I'm interested in paleolithic art," Sally began.

"Can you be more specific?" Casada said. "'paleolithic art' could mean many things."

"Perhaps a bone carving from one of the Cro-Magnon sites in southern France," Sally said.

Casada nodded with a thin smile. "I'm sure I could get one. My sources are numerous—and worldwide. It could be a very expensive piece, however. What kind of money are we talking about?"

"I'm not looking for it for myself. I have a client who is prepared to pay . . . whatever you ask," Sally said.

Otto came back with a tray containing an ornate porcelain teapot, cups, and saucers, placing it on the table.

"The teapot is a Chinese antique?" Sally asked.

"Chien Lung, to be exact," Casada said.

Joe had been gazing at the masks and paintings in the room. "Do you mind if I look around at some of the artwork?" Joe asked.

"Not at all," Casada said.

While Frank, Sally, and Casada continued their discussion, Joe circled the perimeter of the room, pretending to examine the artwork but keeping his eyes open for anything that might be a clue.

As he reached the far wall, he noticed a small office just off the living room. Inside was a desk piled high with folders. Joe casually looked over his shoulder. Otto had left the room, and Frank, Sally, and Casada were still talking. Casada's back was to Joe.

Moving slowly and casually, Joe slipped into the office. Then he quickly thumbed through the folders on the desk. Bingo! One was labeled Cro-Magnon Bison Sculpture.

He eagerly opened the folder and began to finger through the papers inside. Then he stopped. He could feel the back of his neck suddenly turn cold.

Whirling around, Joe drew in a breath. The narrow doorway was completely filled by the hulking figure of Otto.

14 A Prehistoric Trap

The top of Otto's blond crewcut brushed the top of the doorframe. Joe looked up at the huge man. "You will return the folder to the desk," Otto said in a low rumble.

"Oh, this, you mean," Joe said, forcing a smile. "I was just going to take it over to Mr. Casada."

"You will put it back now!" Otto said. He clenched his meaty hands into fists. Joe figured it might be better not to argue.

Joe turned to put the file on the desk. With his body hiding the action, he slipped his hand into the folder. There were several small sheets of paper inside. Joe slipped them out and under his sweater, then turned back, still smiling.

"Thank you. We will now return to the living room." Otto moved from the doorway.

Joe sheepishly did as Otto ordered. Otto stepped ahead, pausing to whisper in Casada's ear.

Casada's eyes narrowed and he stood up. "I've just been informed that one of you has abused my hospitality. I do no business with those I do not trust. Otto will see you to the door."

Sally and Frank got up, both of them flashing Joe a look. "Well, I guess my client will have to look elsewhere for his artifact," Sally lamented.

Casada gazed at her coolly. "I'd be careful, young lady. Pretending to be something you're not can lead to . . . difficulties."

Otto held the door. Joe, Frank, and Sally hurried out to Sally's car.

"Make it quick, Sally," Joe said. "Man-mountain Otto may change his mind about letting us leave so easily."

Sally started the car and zipped down the driveway. As the gate opened automatically, Sally let out a relieved sigh. "Am I ever glad to get out of there," she said, turning onto the road. "That Casada guy gave me the creeps."

Frank turned around to Joe in the back seat. "What did you do to get on Otto's bad side?"

Joe grinned and reached under his sweater, producing the papers he had removed from Casada's office. "These were in a folder on Casada's desk filed under Cro-Magnon Bison Sculpture."

Frank shuffled through the slips of paper. "Uh-huh. This is a bill of sale for a paleolithic bison sculpture," he announced. "And it's signed by a Gwen Flanders and Clarence Smith."

"Who's Gwen Flanders?" Joe asked.

Sally thought for a moment. "She's called for Dr. Smith a few times," she said. "And remember when I first tried to introduce you to Smith and he was arguing with a woman in his office? I think that was Gwen Flanders. I've never met her, but I saw her name in Smith's appointment book."

Joe snapped his fingers. "The redhead on the beach! There was a woman with Casada the other night. I thought she looked familiar."

"I'll bet she's the go-between on Casada's dirty deals," Frank said. "With his shady reputation, he'd need someone to front for him."

"But this receipt only shows that Smith bought the sculpture," Sally pointed out. "He could have bought it not knowing it was fake."

Frank shook his head. "Remember how Smith tossed the broken sculpture pieces into a bag? As a former paleontologist, he'd have been trained to handle them more carefully," Frank said.

"Unless he knew they were fake," Joe said.

Sally sighed. "I guess I just don't want to believe that Dr. Smith would be involved in the purchase of a forgery." She was silent for a moment. "That sculpture was part of Elsa Mansfield's exhibit. Do you think she had anything to do with it?"

"My guess is that Smith bought it in her absence," Frank said.

Sally reached for the receipt. "It's dated May fifteenth. Elsa had left on her expedition by then." She frowned. "And Lubski was away at a conference that week. Smith must have just added it to the collection."

"Where does Smedly fit into this?" Joe asked.

"Smith could have sent him to Casada's, perhaps to set up a new purchase," Frank said.

"Smedly negotiating a deal?" Joe said skeptically. "Forget it."

"Maybe he was just delivering a message. That's not our problem right now. We need to get Smith out in the open." Frank smiled faintly. "And I think I know a way. Let's find Parker."

Back at the museum, Frank, Joe, and Sally headed straight for the dinosaur park. Parker was hunched over a computer monitor in the control shack. After hearing what happened at Casada's, he asked, "How are you going to trap Smith?"

"You may not like it," Frank said. "It involves getting Lubski to help us."

Parker groaned. "Lubski? Give me a break."

"Hear me out," Frank said. "We explain the situation to Lubski. Then we get him to go tell Smith he thinks the bison sculpture was a phony."

"What next?" Parker asked.

"We hope Smith panics and does something foolish," Frank said.

"If you want to scare Smith, Lubski's your man," Parker admitted. "With Elsa Mansfield gone, he's the closest thing we've got to an expert on paleo-lithic art. I know zero about it."

"So how did you figure that the bison sculpture was a forgery?" Sally asked.

Parker laughed. "Something I learned in Paleontology 101. If the surface of an object looks old but the inside looks fairly recent, somebody's trying to slip a fake past you."

"What are we waiting for?" Sally said. "Let's go talk to Lubski."

Parker nodded. The four of them headed to the fossil lab. Lubski looked up in surprise as Sally stepped up to him. "Do you have a minute, Carl?" she said. "We have a proposition for you."

"A proposition?" Lubski repeated, eyeing Parker skeptically.

"We need your help to clean up things around here." Frank described their visit to Casada's and the discovery of the receipt. He then asked the paleontologist if he'd talk to Smith.

Lubski actually smiled. "Of course," he said. "I've had my suspicions for a while."

"In the meantime, how about a truce between you and Dan?" Sally said.

Lubski and Parker looked at each other sheepishly, like two feuding schoolboys. "Oh, fine," Lubski said, a little embarrassed.

"No problem," Parker said.

"Then let's go," Frank said.

"Right now?" Lubski said.

"You have a good chance of catching Smith in his

office now," Frank said. "We'll wait for you here in the lab."

Fifteen minutes later, Lubski was back.

"How did it go?" Sally asked.

Lubski sat in his well-worn chair. "I told Smith that I suspected the bison sculpture had been a forgery, and I wanted a piece for testing." Lubski said. "He grew very upset, though he tried not to show it. But he stammered, pacing around his office. He told me not to worry about it, he'd already planned to have the remnants tested."

"Carl Lubski, the actor," Sally teased. "Who knew?"

The older man grinned. "What now?" he asked.

"My guess is that he'll try to get rid of the bison pieces permanently," Frank said.

"But doesn't he need them for the insurance company?" Sally asked.

"But now he may worry that the insurance company will have them tested," Joe said.

"How can he get rid of them?" Parker asked.

"I don't know," Frank admitted. "He wouldn't dispose of them in his office. That would leave traces too close to him. I can't see him going too far from the administrative wing."

"I bet he'll try it tonight," Joe said.

"He can wait until after the museum closes," Parker said.

"So how will we catch him?" Lubski asked.

Frank looked at his watch. "It'll be closing time in about an hour. We'll all seem to leave, but we'll

141

just park our cars off by the woods behind the museum. Then we'll come back and keep a close watch on the grounds from the cover of the trees."

Parker frowned. "A long shot, maybe, but it's as good as anything I can think of." Sally and Lubski also agreed.

Leaving one by one, the five drove their cars around the side road and into the woods. Then they followed the path through the woods that Frank and Joe had scouted out in their previous secret visits. They crouched in the bushes a short distance from the administrative wing of the old mansion.

"We may have blown it," Sally said in a low voice. "He might have just destroyed the bison fragments inside."

"I think he'll wait till he's sure everyone has gone," Frank said. He put his high-powered binoculars to his eyes, scanning the whole building. There was no movement for at least ten minutes.

"This may just be a wild-goose chase," Lubski said.

"Be patient, Carl," Sally said.

"Wait a minute. Here we go," Frank said, looking through the binoculars. "Smith just came out the door of the fossil wing, holding a bag. I'll bet it's the bison fragments."

They all poked their heads through the bushes. Frank passed the binoculars around so everyone could get a look.

Joe watched as Smith went to the site of the wrecked workshop. Construction workers had dug a

142

large hole there, creating a foundation for the replacement building. Smith emptied his bag into the hole, then dumped several bags of quick-drying cement into a nearby trough. He used a hose to add water, then a shovel to mix the ingredients. As Smith paused for a moment, Joe whispered, "Time to make our move. He's about to bury the pieces."

Frank and Joe led the small group from the cover of trees and bushes and ran toward the director. Smith was stirring the cement, breathing hard and concentrating on his task. In the twilight, he didn't see the Hardys and the others marching up on him.

"Getting rid of the evidence?" Lubski blurted out.

Smith jumped at the voice, dropping his shovel. "Wha—who?" He looked in surprise from face to face. "Evidence? What are you talking about?"

Joe pointed to the hole. "The evidence you're covering up with that cement," he said.

"I—I don't know what you're talking about." Smith stepped in front of the hole as if he could hide what he'd been doing.

"Dr. Smith," Sally said sadly, "we all saw you throw the bag of bison fragments into that hole. Why else would a museum curator be laying a foundation?"

"I—ah—" Smith tried to laugh, an awful sound. "Don't be silly," he said. "I suggest you all go home, and we can discuss this tomorrow."

"Burying won't work," Frank said. "We have Casada's invoice with your signature on it."

143

"And we've already tested one of the bison fragments," Parker added. "We know the sculpture was a fake."

Smith looked frantically from Parker to Frank to Sally. He took a step forward, then back, like a trapped animal. Finally, he turned back toward the museum and began to run.

"Frank!" Joe yelled. "He's getting away!"

15 Cover-Up Uncovered

Frank lunged for the director. As he did, Smith tried to leap out of the way. But his feet got tangled in the water hose snaking across the ground, and he fell headfirst into the hole.

Smith's head and body disappeared. Only his two feet were left sticking above the surface.

Frank and Joe rushed over. Frank grabbed one ankle, Joe, the other. "Pull on the count of three," Frank said. "One, two, three!"

They yanked on the director's legs and pulled Smith from the hole and dragged him onto the ground. His head and face were completely covered with mud.

"I'll wash him off!" Sally said, rushing to get the hose lying on the ground. Turning the nozzle to spray, she aimed the water at Smith's head.

"Agh!" he gasped as the cold water hit him. He sat up, coughing. Using the hose and Lubski's handkerchief, Sally managed to get Smith's face sufficiently cleaned off so he could talk.

"Are you all right now?" she said.

"Of course n—not," Smith sputtered, shivering from his cold bath.

"Let's go to your office and talk," Frank said. "We don't want you to freeze."

Smith stood up and tried to straighten his now filthy, wet shirt. Then he strode back to his office with as much dignity as he could muster. The others followed him.

Smith sank into the chair behind his desk. Water began dripping off him to form a puddle around him.

"All right," he confessed in a tight voice. "Those *were* the bison fragments I was burying. I admit I've done some terrible things, but they were all for the museum." He stared bleary-eyed from face to face. "You've got to believe me."

The director cleared his throat. "In Elsa Mansfield's absence, I bought that bison sculpture from Gwen Flanders. I should have known that when a deal seems too good to be true, watch out. The piece was still very expensive, but it was a bargain as the market for these things goes. Flanders gave me a certificate of authenticity, of course, but I later found out the piece was a forgery. I had no idea at the time that she was working for Casada."

"So you didn't know it was a fake when you bought it," Frank said.

"Not at all," Smith said. "I found out by accident that Casada was the one behind the deal. Too late, I started getting suspicious. I scraped off a tiny bit of the sculpture and had it tested anonymously by an independent laboratory."

He sighed. "After I knew it was a fake, I decided the bison had to be destroyed 'accidentally.' Then, I could hide the fact that it was a fake and still recover the loss to the museum with the insurance money."

"And that's when you got Smedly involved," Joe said.

"Yes. The biggest mistake of my life," Smith groaned. "Each time he attempted to destroy the sculpture, he only made things worse. And he went far beyond what I told him to do. He was only supposed to get rid of the sculpture, not jeopardize anyone's life."

"Smedly ran our van off the road with his car," Joe said. "We almost went over an embankment. We could have been killed."

Smith dropped his head into his hands, his eyes squeezed shut. "Believe me," he begged. "He did that completely on his own."

"I'm sure he thought he was doing it for you," Sally put in. "How did you get him to go along with your scheme to destroy the bison in the first place?"

"When I first hired Smedly, I didn't bother to

147

check his references," Smith said. "It didn't seem that important at the time. When I finally *did* check his references, I found that he had lied about his previous jobs. He was fired from most of them for carelessness or incompetence. When this problem with the bison piece came up, I realized that I could basically blackmail him into helping me."

"So Smedly became a pawn in your hands," Lubski said.

"Yes, Carl," Smith said. "I also took advantage of the rivalry between you and Dan. I hoped that the destruction of the bison sculpture would seem like just another prank. I even added fuel to the fire by pulling some of my own pranks on each of you."

"Like the slashed Dinobot the other night?" Frank asked. Smith nodded miserably.

"Why didn't you just return the sculpture to Casada and ask for your money back?" Joe asked.

"I tried," Smith said. "I didn't want to be seen at Casada's, so I sent Smedly over there several times. But Casada just laughed at my request. I decided that destroying the sculpture was the only way out."

Sally shook her head. "So what do we do now?" she said.

"There is nothing that *can* be done," Smith said. "My career is ruined, the museum will never open —and I'll probably go to jail!" The director remained hunched miserably over his desk.

There was silence in the small office, then Parker spoke up. "It might be best if you resigned," he said quietly. "Sackville's trustees can meet to pick a new curator. They don't need to be told about what happened. If all this came out in the press, the scandal would destroy the museum."

Smith nodded. "I agree," he said. "I need a long rest anyway."

There was an awkward silence. Then Lubski said, "Well, I also have a confession to make. I did sabotage Dan's virtual reality device and reprogrammed the Dinobot that grabbed Joe. I only meant to make small changes in his computer programs—just enough to get his goat. I never intended for anyone to get hurt. I'm really very sorry."

Parker's boyish grin spread across his face. "I have to admit, what you did was very sophisticated electronically. Not many people have that kind of expertise."

"Thanks," Lubski said, surprised.

"And I'm not blameless myself," Parker went on. "I switched the fossil bones in your exhibit. And I was planning some other mischief that I hadn't gotten around to yet."

Lubski laughed, and Frank and Joe looked at each other in surprise. "You know, the creatures you invented were rather amusing," Lubski said.

Sally smiled. "The two of you can argue all you want," she said, "but can we keep it on an intellectual level from now on?"

* * *

About a week later, Sally, Parker, and the Hardys met at the diner in Sackville.

"Is the museum almost ready for the opening?" Frank asked.

"Just about," Sally said. "Things are going much smoother now. Elsa Mansfield has returned from India and been put in charge of the museum by the board of trustees."

"And how are you and Lubski getting along?" Joe asked Parker.

"Well, I wouldn't say we're close friends, but we have a new respect for each other," Parker said. "He's even offered to do what he could to get me reinstated in my doctoral program."

"Has anybody heard from Smedly?" Frank asked.

"Not since the day after we caught Smith trying to bury the bison fragments," Sally said. "Just before he left, he claimed that he just wanted to scare you and Joe off. That's why he stopped on the road, to make sure you were all right. In any event, Smedly has disappeared, I assume for good."

"How about Smith?" Joe asked.

"He cleared out his desk and left the next day, too," Sally said. "Elsa Mansfield told me that he went to the Bahamas for a long rest."

"I'm glad everything worked out," Frank said.

"Sally and I want to thank you guys for everything you did," Parker said.

"Yes," Sally said. "Without your help, the museum might not have survived."

"Oh, I almost forgot," Parker said. "Lubski sends

150

his regards—and this, too." He set a small box on the table. "Go ahead and open it," he said.

Frank took the lid off and pulled out a miniature pink plastic Triceratops. Parker touched a switch on the back. The miniature Dinobot began to run in circles, giving out a faint roaring sound.

"More my size—and speed," Joe admitted.

The four of them all burst out laughing.

"If nobody did anything, nothing in the world would be different. Not everyone realizes that kids can make a difference too. Some adults think we can't, but we can."
– 9 year-old girl, talking about volunteering

Help your community!

Get in on the action!

Kids can make a big difference! Nickelodeon's The Big Help campaign gives you the opportunity to help in your community.

- **THE BIG HELP™ Book, by Alan Goodman:** Hundreds of ways—big and small—that you can help. Available wherever books are sold.

- **THE BIG HELP™ Telethon:** This fall, Nickelodeon will air a telethon that asks you and kids across the country to call in and pledge time, not money. Then you can spend the amount of time you pledged helping others.

- **THE BIG HELP™ Day:** A national celebration for kids, parents, and everyone else who participates in THE BIG HELP™

Why Nickelodeon? Nick believes that kids deserve to have their voices heard and their questions answered. Through events like 1992's Kids Pick the President, 1993's Kids World Council, Plan It for the Planet, and now the THE BIG HELP™, Nick strives to connect kids to each other and the world.

A MINSTREL BOOK

Nickelodeon is a registered trademark of MTV networks, a division of Viacom International , Inc.

1010